All London was abuzz with talk about the latest entry in the aristocratic marriage mart—the beautiful, witty and wealthy Miss Elisabeth Henrick.

No one suspected what only Elisabeth and her courtesan aunt Letty knew—that only a short time before, Elisabeth had been the humble governess Harriet Tremaine.

Even the dashing Mr. Darnell Somerton, who had pursued and been rebuffed by the straitlaced Miss Tremain, was blinded to the truth as he fell under Elisabeth's spell and asked her to be his bride.

How could Elisabeth turn her back on this gentleman who had won her heart? Yet how could she enter into what the world thought a perfect marriage and what would really be a perilous masquerade. . . ?

THE MYSTERIOUS GOVERNESS

Ø

Delightful Regency Romances from SIGNET

THE MYSTERIOUS GOVERNESS

April Kihlstrom

A SIGNET BOOK

NEW AMERICAN LIBRARY

NAL BOOKS ARE AVAILABLE AT QUANTITY DISCOUNTS
WHEN USED TO PROMOTE PRODUCTS OR SERVICES.
FOR INFORMATION PLEASE WRITE TO PREMIUM MARKETING DIVISION,
NEW AMERICAN LIBRARY, 1633 BROADWAY,
NEW YORK, NEW YORK 10019.

SIGNET TRADEMARK REG. U.S. PAT. OFF. AND FOREIGN COUNTRIES
REGISTERED TRADEMARK—MARCA REGISTRADA.
HECHO EN CHICAGO, U.S.A.

SIGNET, SIGNET CLASSIC, MENTOR, PLUME, MERIDIAN AND
NAL BOOKS are published by New American Library,
1633 Broadway, New York, New York 10019

First Printing, April, 1984

1 2 3 4 5 6 7 8 9

PRINTED IN THE UNITED STATES OF AMERICA

—1—

Mr. Somerton deliberately raised his quizzing-glass and surveyed the docks with an air of impatience and exasperation. From the swiftness with which he dropped the glass again, it was to be inferred that Mr. Somerton found nothing to please him in the scene that met his eyes. There was, moreover, a look of strength and determination about the man that caused the dockhands to give him a wide berth. It was something to which Mr. Darnell Somerton was accustomed. From the shine on his top boots to the fit of his breeches and the cut of his coat, from the care with which his short dark curls were arranged, everything about Mr. Somerton proclaimed him a member of the British *ton* and a man who was accustomed to having his own way.

Abruptly Mr. Somerton's air of exasperation left him and he moved forward with surprising speed. A touch of his cane here, a word there, and he had soon reached the side of a young woman heatedly arguing with a dockhand. As was his wont, Mr. Somerton did not hesitate to intervene. "Difficulty, ma'am?" he demanded curtly.

At these words, the woman turned and Darnell Somerton found himself confronted by a pair of large green eyes and a fragile face framed by the severest of brown bonnets. Not a wisp of hair strayed from place nor did the cut of the woman's dress soften her appearance. It was perhaps this that made her voice all the more arresting when she said, liltingly and without the least trace of subservience, "You are very good, sir. This . . . this *person* assured me that if I gave him ten pounds he would arrange passage for me aboard this ship. I was foolish enough to do so and now he claims no knowledge of either my ten pounds or space aboard ship!" There was the barest ghost of a smile about her lips as she added wryly, "You needn't tell me I'm the greatest pea goose alive for trusting the fellow, for I already know as much."

"Then why did you?" Somerton asked, intrigued in spite of himself.

The dockhand started to slip away, and without effort, Somerton seized the fellow's arm and held him while the woman, evidently an abigail, or something of the sort, replied. "I can only plead desperation, sir. I must return to England at once. My . . . my mother has died."

The dockhand again tried to pull free and Somerton decided to deal with him first. A few words were all that were required for the ten pounds to be produced, and as soon as he felt himself set loose, the fellow turned and ran. Darnell shrugged carelessly and presented the money to the young woman with something of a flourish. "You are very good to help me," she told him warmly. "Thank you, Mr.—?"

"Somerton," he replied with the faintest of

bows. "May I ask what your plans are now, Miss—?"

She seemed unaccountably to hesitate before she answered. "Miss Tremaine. My plans? To attempt to return to England, of course."

Mr. Somerton looked down at the determined face of this woman who scarcely reached his chin. "That will be difficult," he told her coolly. "With Boney marching on Brussels and half the British visitors there fleeing homeward, you would need far more than ten pounds to purchase a berth. Whether aboard this or any other ship. Even if you could find one unspoken for, and that I take leave to doubt!"

Miss Tremaine's eyes fell, but a moment later rose once more as she said with quiet courtesy, "Thank you for your frankness, Mr. Somerton. I am sorry to have troubled you."

She turned to go and Somerton stopped her. "Wait!" he said sharply. As she looked at him with startled eyes, Darnell persisted. "Have you anywhere to go? A position to return to?"

Miss Tremaine was pleased to note that there was no more than a trace of unsteadiness in her voice as she replied, "I don't know where I shall go, sir, but I cannot see that it concerns you. I *was* employed as a governess in a Belgian household and I suppose I could return there. But I won't. I shall continue to try to find a way to get back to England."

Darnell Somerton smiled a smile that ought to have dazzled anyone, and most surely a mere governess. "Perhaps I can help you," he said smoothly. "I have booked passage on the *Golden Mermaid* and I think a place could be found for you."

The smile which should have dazzled Miss

Tremaine did not do so. Instead, she drew herself stiffly erect and spoke in measured tones. "I suppose I have left myself vulnerable to such offers, Mr. Somerton, but I am not yet so desperate as to accept one. I am sorry if I have misled you into believing otherwise. Good day, sir."

Darnell was amused and it showed in the crinkling of his eyes. His voice, however, was grave as he replied. "You have mistaken my intent, Miss Tremaine. I did not think you would accept a dishonourable offer, nor was I attempting to make you one." He paused and allowed a condescending smile to appear. "Believe me, Miss Tremaine, you vastly over-rate your attractiveness! Perhaps it will set your fears at rest if I explain that I am escort-ing my sister-in-law back to England. She is breeding and my brother cannot accompany her himself. He is with Wellington's staff, you know. What I thought, Miss Tremaine, was that my sister-in-law might welcome an-other female about her and that you would be glad of a means home. I am sorry if I was mistaken, but you did say you were desperate."

There was no mistaking the amusement in his voice, and Miss Tremaine coloured deeply. She did not, however, compound her folly by attempting to apologise, and after a moment, Somerton demanded sharply, "Well? Do you wish to take passage with my party or not?"

Startled, Miss Tremaine replied vehemently, "Yes! Most certainly, yes!"

"Good. Then come along," he said curtly. "Where are your things?"

"Here," she answered, pointing to the box at her feet. "I haven't very much, you see."

"How fortunate," Somerton said dryly. "Particularly in view of how much my sister-in-law has seen fit to bring along. And in view of the fact that our ship is due to set sail any time now."

It was but a moment's effort to find a boy to carry Miss Tremaine's box, and they set off rapidly for the *Golden Mermaid*. Along the way, Somerton spoke only once, and that was to tell Miss Tremaine, "I advise you to stay aboard, however long we are delayed here. I shouldn't wish the ship to sail without you."

"You needn't fear," Miss Tremaine told him bluntly, "neither should I."

Mr. Somerton's words were unnecessary. Miss Harriet Tremaine had no intention of casting off the opportunity chance had thrown her way. She only hoped that there was, indeed, a sister-in-law. For Harriet Tremaine was not unaware of the risk she took in accepting a strange gentleman's offer. As she had told him, however, her situation seemed desperate. In this, Miss Tremaine was scarcely unique: many of her fellow passengers would have claimed the same. But it was not Bonaparte that concerned Miss Tremaine, rather it was the letter she had tucked safely into her reticule.

Dear Harriet,
    Urgent that you return home at once. Your mother has died and left you a respectable competence. Urgent that you put forth your claim for this inheritance here in England.

                              Ever yours,
                              Letitia

That brief epistle, so unlike her aunt's usual rambling letters, had resulted in a sympathetic dismissal from her employer and a bonus with her wages. Which, had it not been for this mad scramble to purchase passage back to England, must have been more than sufficient for Miss Tremaine's needs. Under the circumstances, however, every innkeeper and ship's captain hereabouts had raised prices.

As the wind blew her skirts, Miss Tremaine almost laughed. She was not, she knew, a vision of loveliness. To imagine that she could inspire passion in such a noted member of the *ton* as Mr. Darnell Somerton was indeed ludicrous. But then, when one was a governess, one's position was far safer if men thought of one as a brown wren rather than as a bird of paradise!

Abruptly Mr. Somerton's voice broke into her reverie. "Here we are, Miss Tremaine. Woolgathering? We haven't time for it, you know. I've got to take you to my sister-in-law's cabin and introduce you. So come along and mind your footing. The deck is quite filthy in places!"

Meekly Miss Tremaine did as she was bid. The past five years had taught her to make the best of her lot as well as the value of silence when one was quite wishing to give someone a sharp set-down.

The cabin was soon reached and Miss Tremaine was presented to Mrs. Olivia Somerton. To her great relief, Miss Tremaine found herself subjected only to the briefest of scrutiny. It was evident that Mrs. Somerton was not finding her journey an easy one, and Harriet guessed that they would not be long at sea before the lady became ill. None of this showed on Miss Tremaine's face, however, as she made her curtsey and answered Mrs. Somerton's questions. "Yes, ma'am, I am British and have been in service in Belgium these past ten months as governess to a family I had worked for in London. Yes, ma'am, I have only just met Mr. Somerton. My mother has died and I must return home at once. Mr. Somerton was kind enough to offer to help me."

At this point Mr. Somerton intervened to say, in a rather bored voice, "Perhaps I ought to assure you, Olivia, that I have no designs upon Miss Tremaine's virtue."

Mrs. Somerton smiled at her brother-in-law. "And if you did have, you would say it was none of my affair!"

He shrugged. "Let us say I should consider any such questions impertinent. Under the circumstances, however, you are merely distressing Miss Tremaine. Need we force her to feel more uncomfortable than is necessary on this journey?"

"Of course not!" Olivia agreed spiritedly. Impulsively she held out a hand. "Forgive me, Miss Tremaine. It is simply that I could not resist roasting my brother-in-law. But I should have to be an utter featherbrain to fear he could be pursuing you!"

Faced with the deceptively frail-looking, fair-haired woman before her, Miss Tremaine could not resist smiling. Then with a curtsey and a twinkle in her eyes that belied the demureness of her voice, Miss Tremaine replied, "Oh, ma'am, I cannot think of any gentleman who has ever so far forgotten himself as to approach me with improper proposals. Or, indeed, to offer any insult to my person whatsoever. I think it must be as my mother was used to say: virtue is its own protection!"

Olivia Somerton looked at her brother-in-law with speaking eyes as she nodded to Miss Tremaine. Mrs. Somerton's abigail, however, who was herself an extremely plain woman, said judiciously, "Just so." Then, with a sort of grudging kindness, she added, "If you would be wishing to place your things over here, miss, they would be out of the way."

Before Harriet could reply, Somerton spoke. "Let me move that box for you, Miss Tremaine."

"*Such* a gentleman!" Olivia could not resist teasing him.

"Just so," Darnell agreed affably. "In point of fact, I am so much the gentleman, my dear Olivia, that I shall take Miss Tremaine for a walk on deck so that you may have her out of your way for a bit. Come along, Miss Tremaine!"

This last command, uttered so peremptorily, allayed whatever lingering fears Olivia might have had about her brother-in-law's interest in the governess. It was impossible to imagine anything less loverlike than his manner with her, or any creature less likely to suit Darnell's tastes. He was a man far too fond of beauty and passion for that! No, Olivia thought with affection, it was just like Darry to be so thoughtful as to take the governess aboard ship and then to take her for a turn about the deck. He knew Olivia well enough to guess she would find it a bore to converse with such a drab little mouse. And then, in the next moment, the baby moved inside Olivia, kicking hard, and she lost all thought of Miss Tremaine.

The drab little mouse was equally grateful that she need not converse with Mrs. Somerton. She far preferred the silent company of Mr. Somerton. After several minutes of this silence, however, Darnell casually said, "You are very quiet, Miss Tremaine. Are you thinking of England, or of the post you've just left?" It was not what he had meant to say. But faced with this so serious woman by his side, he found he could not bring himself to demand of her the questions that filled his head when he looked at her or listened to her speak.

Unaware of his thoughts, Harriet forced herself to look at Somerton and smile. He seemed intolerably close to her, intolerably handsome, and the sea breeze ruffled his hair as her fingers longed to do. It was an experience to which she was totally unaccustomed, and with a lightness she did not feel, she replied, "Why, England, of course! I have only been away ten months, but it feels far longer."

As she spoke, something seemed to catch in Harriet's throat. Ten months since I last saw England, five years since I last saw home, she thought, and no guarantee that I shall not have to leave it all over again.

Something of this must have shown in her face, for Darnell immediately asked, "Is something wrong, Miss Tremaine?"

Harriet sighed and shook her head. "You are far to perceptive, Mr. Somerton!"

"Will you tell me about it?" he invited kindly.

For the briefest moment Harriet's eyes met his, then fell as she realised how impossible it was and yet how close she had come to doing so. Too dangerous! she warned herself urgently. And yet there was a part of her that would have spoken, and to the devil with the risk! Instead, Miss Tremaine spoke quietly and in a voice that scarcely trembled as she said, "I cannot, Mr. Somerton."

"Your mother, I collect," he said wisely. "I shall leave you to your grief," he added, and strolled away, suddenly unaccountably eager to be away from there.

Even then, aware as she was of the impossibility of doing so, Harriet might have called him back had she not been so stunned by his unexpected departure. Nevertheless, it was better that way, she told herself as she turned to the railing and looked out over the water. Furiously she scolded herself. Just why should you be upset that he is gone? You know you are far safer this way! And soon her thoughts did go back to her home and mother and the years and events that separated her from both.

So intent was Miss Tremaine upon her thoughts that she scarcely noticed the sky growing overcast. Nor did she even hear the captain approach sometime after that. "Ma'am? There's a storm brewing and you'd best be going below," he told her grimly.

Harriet spoke hastily. "Must I? So soon?"

"Aye, ma'am. I'll not be having females on deck with the wind blowing up the way she is. I want you all stowed safely below so that I needn't keep my mind on the passengers when I'm needing it to see to the ship."

Harriet nodded, a sense of panic closing in on her. The captain's next words did not allay her fear. "Here comes a gentleman. Be he with your party?"

Before she could reply, Mr. Somerton's voice called out above the rising wind, "Miss Tremaine! May I escort you below? I am afraid you will soon find the weather most unpleasant up here."

Harriet bit her lower lip, knowing she could

scarcely refuse. Reluctantly she said, "Very well, though I assure you I am, in general, an excellent sailor."

At her hesitation, Darnell drew his brows together and said, with a trace of impatience, "So am I, but that is beside the point! For my comfort, if not yours, I beg you will come below now so that I need not fetch you later."

Harriet coloured, knowing his words to be entirely justified. She gathered her skirts with one hand and nodded. "Very well, Mr. Somerton. Captain, I shall be out of your way in a trice."

Ignoring Mr. Somerton's proffered arm, Harriet headed for the nearest hatch. Darnell followed, a most thoughtful expression on his handsome face. As soon as they were belowdeck, he took her arm and said, "This way, Miss Tremaine."

But Miss Tremaine was scarcely so green as to agree without protest. She stood quite still and said slowly, "Do you know, it is quite odd of me, Mr. Somerton, but I distinctly recall that your sister-in-law's cabin was in the opposite direction."

"Still frightened of me, Miss Tremaine?" Somerton asked with an uncharacteristic drawl. "You needn't be, you know." She still did not move, and after a moment, he sighed and went on, "You are quite correct, Miss Tremaine. My sister-in-law's cabin *is* the other way. Olivia finds herself, however, feeling rather indisposed at the moment and would much prefer not to be disturbed. I see nothing for it, therefore, but to take you to my cabin. But you have nothing to fear, I assure you! I should never dream of disarranging my neckcloth, tied with

such exquisite intricacy, you see, by making
improper advances to you." In spite of herself,
Harriet Tremaine gave a gurgle of laughter.
"Much better!" Somerton told her approvingly.
"Now let us go on to my cabin."

This time Harriet did not resist the hand at
her elbow and they reached the cabin just as
the ship began to roll alarmingly. Once inside,
Somerton directed an anxious look at his guest
and said, "I hope you are indeed an excellent
sailor, Miss Tremaine, for I fear we are in for a
rather unpleasant voyage."

She laughed. "Never fear, Mr. Somerton, I
shan't put you to the embarrassment of deal-
ing with a female in dire distress. I only hope
your fortitude is equally reliable!"

Darnell smiled briefly at her teasing tone
but hesitated before he spoke. "You know, Miss
Tremaine, I find you quite remarkable for a
governess."

Abruptly Harriet's amusement left her and
once more she felt the sense of panic close
over her. As she watched, Somerton casually
crossed his arms and leaned his broad back
against the door as he waited for her reply.
With an effort Harriet laughed again and said,
"Do you? Then I must conclude you have been
acquainted with very sorry members of my
profession." Darnell refused to answer and
merely watched her. Waiting. After a moment,
rather nettled, Harriet went on, "If you doubt
my credentials, Mr. Somerton, I can furnish
you with the names of my employers for the
past five years."

It was a bold stroke, one that Darnell dismissed with a careless wave of his hand. "And
before that?" he asked coolly.

Harriet tried to meet Somerton's eyes and discovered that she could not. "Before that?" she asked, turning away to look out the tiny porthole. "I cannot think it the least importance for you to know."

"Nevertheless I have asked you." Somerton's voice came from directly behind Harriet, and she was not surprised when, a moment later, he placed his hands on her shoulders and turned her to look up at him. Gently he said, "Was it so terrible, then, that you fear to tell me? An indiscretion, perhaps, you fear to have revealed?"

Harriet forced herself to pull free. Pacing about the small cabin, she said vehemently, "It is none of your affair! You have no right to ask me!"

Unperturbed, Darnell watched her. "So it was an indiscretion," he drawled.

Abruptly Harriet stopped pacing and faced him. "Well, there you are out, sir! Whatever my actions have been, they were *not* the result of a youthful indiscretion on my part!"

Somerton drew his brows together as he frowned. "Whatever your actions?" he repeated thoughtfully. "Now, what the devil does that mean?"

"Nothing!" she retorted hastily. "A figure of speech, nothing more!"

"No?" Somerton demanded with a harsh laugh as he bore down on her.

Backing away, Harriet stammered, "K-keep away from me or I shall scream!"

Somerton raised an eyebrow in disbelief. "I doubt it," he said frankly. "I can think of nothing that would more surely ruin your reputation."

Once more Harriet sought refuge in the role of the prudish spinster that she had played in Mrs. Somerton's cabin. With outraged dignity she sniffed, "You must have very odd notions, sir, if you believe I should place my reputation above the danger of being ravished!"

It was enough. Somerton halted and blinked in astonishment. "Danger of being ravished?" he demanded incredulously. Then his expression changed and he smiled sardonically. "Doing it much too brown, Miss Tremaine. You are obviously a most respectable young woman. And yet a most respectable young woman who truly suspected me of such intentions would never have taken such risks as you have done today."

Suddenly anger washed away prudence, and her voice shaking with rage, Harriet retorted, "You are a sanctimonious gudgeon, Mr. Somerton! How dare you try to judge my circumstances? We women do not always have the luxury of playing tamely at propriety all our lives. Some of us must take such risks simply to survive, but that does not change who we are inside!"

Harriet concluded in a burst of tears. Somerton, who had listened with a frown of intense concentration on his face, found himself reaching out and drawing Miss Tremaine's head against his chest. His arms closed comfortingly around her and it occurred to neither of them just how strange such a scene was. A member of the *ton* simply does not console a mere governess in such an extraordinary manner. And, indeed, matters shortly became more extraordinary still.

Harriet ceased shaking, at last, and raised

her head to pull herself free. As she did so, Somerton looked down and their eyes met. Slowly, so that she might have time to protest, Darnell's face descended until his lips closed over hers, and he kissed her. And Harriet did not resist! Instead, she found herself responding with a warmth she had not known she possessed. When at last Somerton released her, Harriet trembled with astonishment and shame. She managed to say, finally, in a creditably cool voice, "I suppose you are amused, sir. May we have done, however, with such foolish games?"

Somerton was a man of thirty years and one who could scarcely be considered a green boy. He dropped his hands from Miss Tremaine's shoulders. "Games?" he asked pointedly. "I should not have said you were entirely indifferent to me, just now."

Mortified, Harriet flushed, forcing herself to meet his eyes. "No, I was not indifferent, Mr. Somerton," she admitted frankly. "And I am quite aware that I have sunk myself beneath reproach. But what has happened here, just now, is best forgotten. Whatever I felt, I am no light-skirt to allow a man to give me a slip on the shoulder." She paused, then forced herself to go on. "I am aware I have given you cause to believe otherwise, but nevertheless it is the truth."

"What you have given me cause to believe," Somerton said quietly, "is that you are not accustomed to being kissed."

Harriet looked at him in astonishment. "How can you possibly know that?" she demanded.

Somerton was amused. "My dear girl, believe

me when I say that I have experience enough
to be sure!"

As Harriet continued to stare at Somerton,
there was a knock at the door. A frown creased
Darnell's brow as he called out, "Who is it?
What do you want?"

In answer, the cabin door opened to reveal
the loveliest woman Harriet had ever seen.
"Darry dearest!" the lady exclaimed.

Harriet could feel Somerton stiffen beside
her. After a long pause he drawled, "Your
Grace, the Duchess of Carston. I am honoured,
but cannot conceive what you are doing here."

The duchess pouted as she stepped forward,
closing the cabin door behind her. "Oh, Darry,
you still have not forgiven me for marrying
George, have you? Never mind, you will! But
forgive me, Darry, I see you are not alone.
Dallying with servants? I had not thought you
so desperate! Especially such a plain thing as
this one is."

Harriet held her breath at the malice in the
woman's voice. Not willingly would she cross
swords with the Duchess of Carston. Somerton,
however, was not so reluctant. There was a
tightness to his voice as he replied, "And I had
no notion *you* were so vulgar, Pamela dear."

The duchess tapped her foot impatiently.
"Well? Aren't you going to tell me who she
is?"

"No."

One look at Somerton's face was sufficient
to see that he meant what he said. Whatever
her intentions had been, it was now borne in
upon the duchess that retreat was the only
course open to her. After a moment she even
managed to smile. "Very well. I shall leave you

to your bit of muslin, Darry. Good-bye, my
dear, I hope you have more luck in pleasing
him than I did."

Somerton waited until the duchess was gone,
then he turned to Harriet and said gravely,
"I'm sorry, Miss Tremaine. I would not have
had you exposed to such unpleasantness if I
could have prevented it. Please believe that
you need not regard anything the duchess has
said." He paused, then went on, "As for what
occurred earlier, please believe that I am not
in the habit of forcing myself upon young
women, and I apologise."

Swiftly Harriet replied, "I do not regard it.
Indeed, I believe the matter best forgotten."

Darnell nodded. With a slight bow he said,
"It would be as well, perhaps, if you return to
my sister-in-law's cabin. I shall see you when
the ship docks. Can you find your way?"

"I believe so," she answered in a voice de-
void of all emotion.

Wordlessly, Darnell held open the cabin door
for Miss Tremaine and watched as she disappeared down the long passage. She seemed painfully fragile to him as she put out her hand to
steady herself with each sharp roll of the ship.
When she was out of sight, he quietly closed
the cabin door.

As for Harriet, she was grateful simply that
matters were not worse. Fortunately for her,
Olivia Somerton took the reappearance of the
governess in remarkably good humour, consider-
ing the state of her physical health. The storm
might, by a seaman's standards, have been a
moderate one, but Olivia had had quite enough
of its effects. Beyond a murmured "oh, there
you are," Mrs. Somerton could not bring her-

self to carry on any sort of conversation. A circumstance for which Miss Tremaine was devoutly grateful. Mrs. Somerton's abigail was equally reticent, all her attention devoted to her mistress.

Only when the ship reached England and the *Golden Mermaid* had settled in her berth did Olivia Somerton begin to feel more herself again. "Have you anyone to meet you here?" she asked Harriet.

Bobbing a slight curtsey, Harriet replied, "No, ma'am."

"Well, where are you going?" Olivia persisted.

"London."

"How provoking!" Mrs. Somerton said crossly. "I had hoped you might be going on with us, but my husband's home is some distance south and west of the city. Well, I shall give you our direction, and should you need help in finding another position, perhaps I may be of assistance. Or do you intend to return to Belgium?"

Harriet could not entirely repress a shudder at the notion. "I hope I may never see Belgium again!" she replied fervently.

"Well, as I said, I shall give you my direction and you mustn't hesitate to ask my help if you need it," Mrs. Somerton told her graciously.

"You . . . you are very kind to someone who is a stranger to you," Harriet stammered.

"Faradiddles!" Olivia retorted decisively. "I pride myself that I am an excellent judge of character, Miss Tremaine, as is my brother-in-law, Darry. If we both approve of you, why, then, there is nothing more to be said!"

Once more Harriet felt as though her emotions might overwhelm her. "I—I am not in the way of having people be so kind to me," she said frankly. "I am very grateful to you."

But Olivia Somerton only shook her head. Before she could speak, there was a rap at the cabin door and Darnell's voice could be heard saying curtly, "Olivia? Are you ready to go ashore? The captain is anxious to see us all depart before dark!"

"Very well," she retorted rather sharply. "Send someone for our things."

A few minutes later Somerton returned, and at Olivia's bidding, Harriet opened the door. Darnell ignored her, directing the porter which boxes and trunks to take first. Then he held the door for his sister-in-law and her abigail and Harriet found herself alone with him. Darnell directed a searching look at her as he said, "You are not still . . . overset?"

"Overset but not overcome," Harriet answered as coolly as she was able.

Darnell nodded curtly. "To be sure. I ought not to have expected otherwise. What are your plans now?"

Harriet repeated what she had told Olivia. When she was done, he said, after a moment's reflection, "Once I have settled Olivia at the inn, I shall try to arrange your passage to London."

Somewhat more coldly than she intended, Miss Tremaine replied, "Thank you. I prefer, however, to manage for myself, Mr. Somerton."

"As you will," he answered, mortified.

And so, a few hours later, Miss Harriet Tremaine found herself on the overnight stage and without Mr. Somerton's assistance. She did not regret the cold dreariness of the journey; she had grown accustomed to such discomfort over the past five years. If she felt any regret at all, it was that she had taken such brief leave of Mrs. Somerton, who had, somehow, been most understanding. Nevertheless, Harriet could not entirely suppress a shudder at the swaying of the coach. One might have supposed the driver to be blind or drunk for the number of times he almost overturned the coach that night. It was a most unpleasant journey.

— 2 —

Letitia Roxbury stretched with a purring sound and smiled lasciviously at her companion, who chuckled. "Now I know why they call you La Perdita," he said, tracing a finger down her long, lovely, bare body.

"Why?" she asked mischievously.

Seizing her in his arms, the gentleman replied, "Because once a man has made love to you, his soul is forever lost to your keeping!"

Hungrily he kissed her hair and face and body, hands greedily stroking everywhere. Letitia responded with an eagerness as great as his own. With the ease of years of practice, Letitia chose her moment and swung herself atop her companion. That gentleman found his desire flamed even higher at the sight of her burnished hair hanging down around her face. And for a time he was oblivious to everything else.

Later, as they lay in a companionable silence together, Letitia surveyed the room with satisfaction. It was done in colours of silver and rose with mementos of past lovers everywhere. Not an inexpensive room, but then neither was any other in the little house tucked away in St. John's Wood.

"What are you thinking, Letty?" the gentleman beside her asked.

She turned her head to smile dazzlingly at him. "Of you. And what an extraordinary man you are. Of how deceptive clothes can be and how wicked a lover you are."

"Liar!" he said without rancour. "Nevertheless I adore you for it."

"And I—"

Before she could say more, there was a scratching at Letty's bedroom door. With a very pretty pout to her companion, she pulled a sheet up to cover them, then called, "Yes?"

The door opened to reveal Letty's maid standing with discreetly downcast eyes. With a curtsey she said, "Beg pardon, ma'am, but the gentleman asked that I come and tell him when it was eight of the clock."

Gracefully Letitia raised her eyebrows questioningly at her companion, who nodded genially. "Quite right. Thank you, my dear." To Letty he explained, "I've a wager with young Quimby. My grays against his chestnuts. We're to race this morning. In an hour, in fact."

Demurely Letitia lowered her eyes and said, "Oh, dear, I do hope I haven't hurt your chances."

In answer, the gentleman kissed Letitia soundly and then said, "My dear, this is the best way in the world to prepare for a race. To the devil with sleep when I can have you! But I must be going. Shall I come tonight and tell you if I've won?"

"If?" Letty chided him playfully. "I've no doubt upon the matter! But come and we shall celebrate your victory."

With a laugh the gentleman rose from the bed and, a short time later, was seen to leave the house in remarkable spirits. As soon as he was gone, Letty's maid reappeared. "Ma'am, you've a caller!" she said, a trifle breathlessly.

"A caller?" Letitia repeated, the lack of enthusiasm evident in her voice. "Couldn't you fob him off? Who is it?"

The maid, a quiet woman who had been with Letitia for years, watched as her mistress donned a satin wrapper. "It's not a man, ma'am, it's a *young person*," she said with meaning.

"A young person?" Letitia asked incredulously. Then, as she realised who it must be, she said briskly, "Very well, show her up here."

"Yes, ma'am," the maid agreed, and promptly left to do so.

An observer might have been pardoned for thinking La Perdita mad. As the door opened, several minutes later, to reveal an extremely plain young woman dressed head to toe in brown, Letitia ran forward and enveloped the creature in her arms. "Elisabeth!" she cried.

The young person, quite forgetting her place, responded with equal fervor, saying, "Aunt Letty!"

Behind the pair, Letitia's maid entered the room carrying a breakfast tray with more than enough food for two. "I thought you might both be hungry," she said primly.

Impulsively, the young woman hugged the maid, "Indeed I am, Abby! How thoughtful of you! And how have you been?"

The maid bobbed a curtsey and smiled reluctantly, "Well enough, Miss Elisabeth, as I hope you've been. I'll be going now and leave you to have a comfortable coze with your aunt. Later I'll be back to fetch the tray."

As the door closed behind her maid, Letitia retreated to the bed and patted a chair beside it. "Come and eat, Elisabeth. Always remember to replenish your strength after a long night, my dear. And food is the best thing for it!"

Elisabeth did as she was bid, an impish smile upon her face. "By which I collect you're as successful as ever?" she said.

Letitia smiled complacently. "I like to think so. Though one ought never to take anything as certain. And you? You look so dreadfully shabby!"

With a laugh, Elisabeth looked down at herself and spoke ruefully, "Yes, I do, don't I? But that was the notion, wasn't it?" Then, more seriously, she removed her bonnet, set it aside, and remarked thoughtfully, "You cannot imagine how grateful I shall feel when I know that I need not be obliged to ever seek a post as governess again. You . . . you mentioned an inheritance in your letter. I don't suppose it runs to enough money to answer?"

Briskly Letitia set down her cup of tea and said, "Ah, but it does, my dear! Harriet Tremaine may disappear and never be seen again!"

Elisabeth blinked at her aunt. "How . . . how is that possible?" she asked.

Letitia leaned forward confidingly. "Your grandfather never liked your father, and when your mother married him, your grandfather set up a special trust. Added to when you were born and entirely separate from the usual marriage settlements. Your mother was to have an allowance from the trust during your father's lifetime, and the principal upon his death. As she died first, however, everything comes to you with the sole stipulation that not one farthing is to benefit your father."

"Papa will fight it," Elisabeth said quietly.

"Oh, no, he won't," Letitia answered grimly, "for I have told him very plainly that he shall have me to deal with if he tries!"

Elisabeth could not feel entirely convinced, but she was too fond of her aunt and too tired to argue. Instead, she asked resolutely, "Well, Aunt Letty, what is it I am required to do in order to claim my inheritance?"

"First," Letitia answered firmly, "you are to eat. Then we must dress you in mourning. Mme Suzette was kind enough to make up a few things for you; after we've had our breakfast, you shall try them on. Abby can alter whatever is necessary."

As she filled a small plate with food, Elisabeth nodded. "Yes, of course. And how very thoughtful of you. But . . . but that wasn't quite what I meant."

Elisabeth stopped and looked helplessly at her aunt, who nodded briskly. "Quite right. What you really want to know is where you must go and whom you must see. The answer to that is—you must go home." At the expression of dismay on Elisabeth's face Letitia leaned forward and said, "Yes, I know you must be wishing me at Jericho for saying so, but it is the truth nevertheless. Your mother's solicitors are there and you must appear in person to claim your inheritance. I shall accompany you so that you need have no fear. Your father shan't try anything so long as I am about. Indeed, he may not be there at all."

Elisabeth blinked. "Not be there?"

Letitia leaned back against her pillows with a sour smile upon her face. "Your father has lost no time in consoling himself," she said dryly. "He has purchased a hunting box in the north country and retreated there to *mourn*. With, I believe, the youngest housemaid on your mother's staff. I should be very much surprised if he returns any time soon."

"I see," Elisabeth said gravely. "And once I have claimed my inheritance? I've no taste to stay there, waiting for my father to reappear. Nor am I old enough to set up an establishment for myself without a chaperone. Nor—"

"Nor can you live with me," Letty finished for her. "How well I know it! Indeed, I've given the matter much thought. While you've been in service these past five years, your parents gave out to everyone that you were at your mother's bedside, attempting to nurse her back to health. And as your parents have never encouraged *anyone* to visit them, no one save the servants there know you were gone. And they are all loyal to you. What I propose is that you write to your cousin Hugh Henrick and his wife, Marietta. You could not go to them five years ago, but now the case is different. Ask to stay at their country home while you are in mourning and I've no doubt Marietta will offer to bring you out, next Season, as well!"

"Won't they think it odd I choose not to mourn at home?" Elisabeth asked doubtfully.

Letitia shook her head and said triumphantly, "No, for you shall tell them you cannot bear to stay where your mother spent her last painful years. I swear it is no more than the truth!"

"And if they ask about those last painful years?" Elisabeth said dryly.

"Say that you cannot bear to speak of it."

Elisabeth was quiet for a while. When she spoke, it was with a sigh. "Do you know, Aunt

Letty, I wish there had been some other way, some other choice to make, five years ago."

"Followed in my footsteps, perhaps?" Letitia asked, a twinkle in her eyes. She looked her niece over and said frankly, "You've neither the temperament nor a sufficient lack of scruples for it, my dear!" Then, becoming more serious, she took Elisabeth's hands in hers. "I know you've had a dreadful time of it. But look forward now, the past is done! Banish Harriet Tremaine forever from your mind and become, once more, Elisabeth Henrick. With your hair properly cut and curled and dressed as you should be, no one will ever guess who you once were. I swear it!"

Elisabeth forced herself to smile and nod decisively. "Elisabeth Henrick it is! And not a moment too soon, my dearest of aunts. When do we leave for my family home?"

"Tomorrow." Letty explained, "Abby will need time to alter those dresses for you. Besides," she said, her eyes dancing, "I've a gentleman calling tonight. And I *never* disappoint a gentleman, my dear!"

3

The spring of 1816 promised to be a gay one, which even the gray skies and cold spring rain could not spoil. London was preparing for the Season and for the return of the members of the *ton* from their winter retreats. No talk of war or wounded soldiers would mar the gaiety this year, and mothers seeking husbands for their daughters counted themselves fortunate as more and more officers returned from the continent. Hostesses planned parties without fear that word of a battle would cast a pall of gloom over her guests. And no less a personnage than Lady Sally Jersey had vowed to make this Season a memorable one.

In the drawing-room of his family's principal estate, however, Darnell Somerton was lost in thought, quite indifferent to the approaching festivities. A generous fire blazed in the hearth, casting long shadows on the solid oak wainscotting. Comfortable sofas and chairs and little tables scattered about invited one to linger, and the blue and gold of the furnishings were nicely calculated to put one at ease. It was not surprising, therefore, that the family had chosen to gather here on a cold March afternoon. Or that the milieu was conducive to reflection. No one else was quite so engrossed, however, as Darnell. Indeed, his mother was obliged to speak his name no less than three times before he heard her; his father, the Viscount Langston, snorted, "Manners! You've none of you young puppies any manners anymore! Or am I to assume we see you moping over that female? That duchess, or whatever she may be."

This was sufficient to bring Darnell's attention back to the present. Meeting his father's eyes squarely, he carelessly crossed one neatly clad leg over the other and said coolly, "The Duchess of Carston, father, is the lady I presume you are referring to. So far from moping over her, as you put it, I cannot recall that I have thought of her much at all these past several months."

"Good!" Lord Langston said emphatically. "It's about time you gave up such pointless affairs and were casting about you for a wife!"

For a moment, such a bleak look crossed Darnell's face that both of his parents were taken aback. Rather harshly he replied, "I should give that subject the go-by, if I were you, Father. You might not like the bride I chose."

"Not like her?" Langston demanded. "What's that to the point? I ain't obliged to like the girl, only approve of her! And so long as you don't choose to marry an opera dancer or a cit's daughter, I ain't likely to object."

"And if I chose a governess?" Darnell asked politely.

As the viscount coloured, Lady Langston judged it time to intervene. "Really, Darry! It is too bad of you to roast us like this. I am persuaded you have far too much family feeling and good sense to commit such a folly. Or any other *mésalliance,* for that matter."

Darnell inclined his head toward his mother, but neither agreed nor disagreed. Olivia Somerton, who was seated in a corner chair embroidering handkerchiefs, said mischievously, "Indeed *I* think it most likely that if Darry consents to be leg-shackled at all, it will be to a brown mouse of a thing, someone not in the least what one would expect."

Darnell Somerton turned a quelling stare upon his sister-in-law, who only grinned impishly. As Lord Langston appeared about to succumb to apoplexy, his wife said hastily, "Now, Olivia! You are quite as wretched as Darry! Do be serious, both of you. Darry, your father is quite right—it *is* time you looked about you for a wife. If none of the girls you have met thus far have taken your fancy, there is still no need to despair. Indeed, I have a friend whose daughter is being presented just this year, and I am sure she is the most amiable creature imaginable."

"Mother," Darnell said warningly before she could go on, "I cannot recall how many daughters of friends of yours you have solicited my kindness for, but I assure you it is far too many."

At this point, Lord Langston intervened to ask delicately, "Darry, you . . . you ain't in the line of . . . of boys, are you?"

Darnell suppressed the impulse to laugh outright and instead answered as gravely as he was able, "No, Father, I am not. I assure you my preferences lie with petticoats."

The viscount did not trouble to hide his relief. "That's as well, then," he said gruffly.

"We've never had that sort as family heir and I trust we never will."

Lady Langston, who had been struggling with a strong sense of indignation for several minutes now, demanded, "And what, pray tell me, Darry, was wrong with Lisa Stanton? Or Amanda Crowley? I grant you Anne Pierce had a squint but what else was there to object to about her?"

"Nothing," Darnell agreed shortly. "They were all very well in their own way, but scarcely the sort of woman I can imagine finding myself tenant-for-life with! You know, Mother, you really would be far happier if you gave over trying to matchmake for me."

"Very well," her Ladyship sniffed pettishly. "If you cannot appreciate the girls—all models of propriety, I am sure—then there is nothing more to be said."

A gleam appeared in Darnell's eyes and for the first time he smiled. "Do you know," he said, staring thoughtfully at the fire, "someone once told me that not everyone has the luxury of being a model of propriety."

Langston snorted. "Some light-skirt, no doubt! Aye, and a very convenient philosophy for the girl to have, too, I'd say."

"I'd say it sounds more like the governess," Olivia said cryptically.

Lord Langston twisted around to look at his daughter-in-law. "Will someone please tell me what the devil all this is about a governess? Surely not Miss Allen, she's far too old for Darry."

Olivia smiled demurely, carefully avoiding Darnell's eyes. "No, of course not Miss Allen, This governess is a young woman we met at the dock when we were fleeing Boney's armies. She hadn't passage home to England and Darry rescued her! Brought her along with us, actually, until Dover."

Langston continued to stare at his daughter-in-law, and when it became clear she had nothing more to add, he said somewhat pettishly, "And?"

"And we lost sight of her there," Darnell replied smoothly. "We've not the slightest notion what she is doing now or where she is to be found. Except, of course, that one presumes she is a governess somewhere."

"Hmph," Langston snorted again. "Then there's nothing to the matter? Thought so. And you, my girl, ought to know better than to go stirring us up over such a broth of nothing! Wishful thinking, I've no doubt. Comes from filling your head with rubbishy novels and all."

No one answered the viscount and silence once more settled over the room. Darnell found his thoughts full of the woman he had seen one year before. It was *not*, he told himself firmly, that he was enamoured of Miss Tremaine. He was intrigued. Intrigued that she was so self-assured and possessed dancing eyes she was so careful to hide. Intrigued that she had so easily vanished without a trace once she had reached London. For Darnell had tried to find her. Merely to assure himself, of course, that she was all right. But Miss Tremaine had vanished, simply vanished. No one, beyond telling him that she had walked away from the coach-yard, could say where she had gone. Resolutely and not for the first time, Darnell tried to banish her image from his mind. But he kept remembering her little gurgle of laughter, the tilt of her head when she listened to him, and the sadness that had filled her eyes on deck of the *Golden Mermaid*. It was not that he had forgotten her unrelieved plainness, it was rather that he found it unimportant. And *that* was what disturbed him most about the whole affair! If any of his friends were to get wind of such a thing, his reputation would forever be in shreds. With a sense of desperation that he could not rid her from his mind, Darnell forced himself to speak aloud. He addressed his sister-in-law, knowing very well his question would engage her attention. "How is baby Rebecca, Olivia?"

At once Olivia was all motherly concern. "Dr. Meadows says that Becky is almost over her cold and that he does not despair of seeing her once more her cheerful self again any day now. It is not, as we feared, scarlet fever after all!"

"I should be happier if we still had dear Dr. Wendover," Lady Langston said pensively. "Dr. Meadows seems so very young to me."

"Well, so long as the fellow knows what he is about, that's all that matters," the viscount said brusquely. "But I must say I am pleased to hear Rebecca is out of danger. I've grown somewhat fond of the little thing." As this was rather an extraordinary thing for him to say, no one quite knew what to answer. Fortunately it seemed he did not expect a reply, for he turned to Darnell and said, "By the by, Darry, where did you acquire your new pair of horses? Tattersalls? Sweet-goers, they look to be."

"They are," Darnell confirmed. "I had them off Wharton, and worth every pound I paid.

Robert was green with envy when he saw them."

"I don't know why he should have been," Olivia said crossly as she set aside her needlework. "He brought back three from the continent. Used his prize money after selling out his commission. And now he's out buying a fourth horse!"

Langston, who was actually very fond of his daughter-in-law, said coolly, "The Somertons have always maintained excellent stables and have never begrudged the expense of doing so."

"It isn't the expense," she protested in return, "it's the time he spends on doing so. I swear I feel as though I scarcely see him for his horses."

"You're bored, that's what it is," Lady Langston said placidly. "But don't despair. He'll take you, I wager, to London for the Season, and that will answer nicely." She paused and looked at her eldest son. "I trust you will be going to London as well, Darry?"

"Oh, yes, you must," Olivia said at once. "Like your mama, I am determined to matchmake and I shall find the bride for you or I am much mistaken in the matter."

Darnell smiled. "My dear sister-in-law, you are welcome to try. But I give you ample warning: I shan't feel bound to show even the least courtesy to the poor girl unless I like her. So I warn you to be careful whom you choose. Though why everyone must harp upon the matter is quite beyond me! I assure you I am well aware of my responsibilities and I have no intention of ignoring them. But I cannot understand your sense of urgency that I toss the handkerchief to some green chit."

"I want to see you wed before I die," Langston said bluntly.

Darnell looked his father up and down, then replied coolly, "Of course, sir. But I had no notion you meant to stick your spoon in the wall just yet."

As the viscount's face darkened, her Ladyship said crossly, "Must you use such abominable cant with us, Darry? I collect you mean to say your father seems in tolerably good health. And so he is. But—"

"But nothing!" Langston said sharply. "Our son will go his own way, as he always has. And I suppose it's as well. I should despise the notion of a milksop stepping into my shoes when I am gone. Do as you please, Darry, but recollect that it would please us very much to see you wed."

The smile Darnell gave his father was an affectionate one. "I shall. Indeed, I cannot see how I could forget it when I am sure everyone will be at such pains to remind me!"

His tone was light and good-natured, but that evening after everyone else had retired, the viscount turned to his wife and said, "Do you know, m'dear, I am concerned about that governess. Darry never did confess he was roasting us over the matter."

Placidly her Ladyship replied, "I shouldn't worry. Even were Darry to have a *tendre* for a governess, depend upon it we should discover that she was something quite out of the common way. Recollect that he has always displayed *your* impeccable taste. And recollect further that Olivia said she was the plainest sort of creature imaginable, so that if he is attracted, it is not for the sake of mere beauty.

Indeed, I quite confess a desire to meet the creature, if she exists."

"And I devoutly pray that the need shall never arise!" Langston thundered in return.

"Oh, dear. Suffering from the gout again, are you?" Her Ladyship clucked sympathetically.

"Aye, damme you, but that has absolutely nothing to say to the matter," he retorted angrily. "I shouldn't stand for my son making a damme fool of himself, gout or no gout!"

"Of course not, my dear," his wife replied soothingly. "I simply meant I found the notion most unlikely. And you are most prone to such fears when your foot is troubling you," she concluded, not in the least abashed.

His Lordship merely snorted.

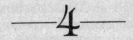

4

London: it was outrageously dirty and noisy or wonderfully exciting, depending upon one's point of view. For Marietta and Hugh Henrick it was *the* place to present their young cousin, Elisabeth, to the *ton*. She was, at twenty-four, a beauty. Rich chestnut curls framed a face that held expressive eyes, a pleasingly shaped nose, and the rosiest of smiles. Neither too tall nor too short, Elisabeth carried herself with grace and assurance. If she was markedly older than other girls making their come-out, she lacked, at least, the simpering missishness of a chit come straight from the schoolroom. Indeed, there was a directness about her that Marietta found, at times, rather disconcerting. As Elisabeth's manners were beyond reproach, however, her cousins had no notion she was anything but the most biddable of girls. It was, to be sure, a trifle awkward that Elisabeth had spent so many years retired in the country, but Marietta did not despair of discovering a creditable match for the girl. Indeed, the vouchers for Almack's had already arrived! No more auspicious omen than the ease with which they had been procured could have been wanted. Marietta said as much, one morning, as they sat over cups of chocolate in Hugh Henrick's London townhouse.

"My dear Elisabeth, Hugh is very pleased. Very pleased indeed. We shall attend the first subscription ball at Almack's tomorrow night and Hugh has consented to accompany us. *That*, you must know, is a very great sacrifice on his part, for he finds these affairs sadly flat! Gentlemen generally do, I am told. But that is neither here nor there. You and I shall enjoy ourselves enormously. I swear it will be as though I myself were once more making my come-out! And, of course, it will be a foretaste of when little Jenny comes of age."

This last was spoken a trifle mournfully and Elisabeth could not help smiling. "We shall indeed enjoy ourselves," she assured her cousin stoutly. "You've no notion how I am looking forward to at last passing through Almack's hallowed portals."

"Well, I am sure I cannot understand why your parents would not allow you to be brought out years ago," Marietta said frankly. "To be sure, your mother's health was too poor to allow of her presenting you herself, but she might easily have permitted someone else to do so." Elisabeth started to speak, but Marietta held up a hand to forestall her. Ruffles fell back from the wrist of her elegant silk dressing gown. "I know, you shall tell me you would have been far too concerned for your mother's health to leave her side! That is all very noble, and I am sure everyone must respect you for it, but it can only have been pure selfishness on the part of your parents to have allowed such a sacrifice. However devoted you may have been to her, and she to you, a nurse must have done just as well."

Marietta paused for breath and Elisabeth regarded her cousin with affection. Marietta was scarcely above thirty years herself, and one of those spritely women everyone seems to adore. Her husband, at forty and after twelve years of marriage, certainly did so. As did her three children. Elisabeth could not help thinking how different matters might have been had it been possible to go to Marietta and Hugh for help when she fled home. But six years ago it had not been possible. Marietta had been carrying her third child and far too close to term to take on the additional burden of her cousin. Indeed, she had almost died in childbirth. Later? Well, later there had seemed no point to it, her role as Harriet Tremaine, governess, so well established.

"You are very quiet," Marietta's voice cut across Elisabeth's thoughts. "I must hope you are not subject to the vapours!"

Elisabeth laughed. "Scarcely! No, I was thinking how fortunate I am to be here, with you and Hugh."

But Marietta would have none of it. "We are fortunate to have you," she told her cousin firmly. "And if you say otherwise, I think I shall take the greatest offence!"

Elisabeth laughed again. "Sorry. My wits must have gone a begging. Tell me, what are your plans this morning?"

Marietta grimaced expressively as she set down her cup of chocolate. "Duty call. You needn't come along unless you wish to. It's my great-aunt Gertrude. A most redoubtable woman, I am sure, but one with the disconcerting way about her of making one feel as if one were still in leading strings! How I wish my family was as intriguing as yours, my dear."

"Do you really think they are?" Elisabeth asked, amused.

Marietta leaned forward and said confidentially, "Well, do you know, I have always longed to be related to someone like your father's half-sister, Letitia Roxbury."

"Not everyone would think it so desirable," Elisabeth said wryly. "I cannot recollect the number of times I have been told that she is my greatest liability! Or that it is a pity my grandfather chose to recognise his natural daughter. I believe it was considered quite eccentric of him to do so."

"And what is that to the point?" Marietta demanded hotly. "I cannot believe it is anything but a credit to your grandfather that he chose to acknowledge his responsibilities! Why should the child have been made to suffer?"

"And yet you have told me I must not recognise Aunt Letty publicly," Elisabeth reminded her gently.

Marietta shifted uneasily in her chair and the gleam of defiance left her eyes as she said, "So I have. And it's no more than the truth. Such a pity! But there is no escaping the fact that your aunt Letty *chose* to follow in her mother's footsteps." A sigh escaped Elisabeth's cousin. "Do you know, I ought not to say this, but I have often wished *I* could acknowledge her. I have always accounted her the most amiable member of your family. Ah, well, what's past mending must be accepted. And now I must dress and be off. Amuse yourself, my dear, while I am out."

Recognising these words as a dismissal, Elisabeth rose and kissed her cousin's cheek. "I hope you have a pleasant morning, Marietta. Perhaps ·ur great-aunt will not be so dreadful after all! Indeed, I cannot see how anyone could ever be other than kind to you."

With a laugh, Marietta waved her young cousin away and rang for her maid. Elisabeth, already dressed, closed the door quietly behind her. In her own room, she paced restlessly, wishing she could be out and about or doing something useful. I am not, she told herself ruefully, accustomed to a life of leisure any longer. Nor to the rules that confine my behaviour now that I am once more the young lady Elisabeth Henrick. In the end, she was reckless. Donning the garments she had worn as Harriet Tremaine, she set out to visit Letty. It was only sentiment that had made her retain these clothes, and she had kept them well hidden so as not to scandalise Marietta's servants. But now they were needed. For however restless Elisabeth might feel, she was not so foolish as to visit Aunt Letty dressed as herself. Were anyone to recognise Miss Elisabeth Henrick doing such a thing, her reputation would be in shreds. When she quietly slipped out of the house, a short time later, she found the streets relatively deserted. At least by members of the *ton*. It was, after all, unfashionably early to be out and about. There was no lack, however, of housemaids and tradespeople and others going about their business. In such a crowd, Miss Harriet Tremaine blended perfectly. Or so she thought.

*   *   *

Mr. Darnell Somerton did not consider the hour to be an early one. Rather, he felt the day to be more advanced than was seemly. His attitude was, perhaps, due to his having missed an appointment to go out riding with a fair charmer he had recently met. Musette was not inclined to be forgiving, even under the best of circumstances; and as Darnell's punctiliousness concerning appointments was something of a jest among his acquaintances, it was not to be expected that Musette would believe he had simply forgotten. Even if she did, moreover, it was unlikely that she would consider poor wine, vehement conversation, and the circumstance of falling asleep in Allenby's chambers to be sufficient excuse for such a lapse in memory. Indeed, Darnell could not account for it himself, and his temper was consequently at its worst this morning. As for his appearance, the most inadequate of valets in London would have been horrified at seeing his master abroad in rumpled evening clothes at the hour of nine o'clock in the morning. Why he had declined to take a hack and had, instead, chosen to walk home was simply one more matter Darnell could not explain.

Under the circumstances, therefore, it is astonishing that Somerton noticed the lady at all. But he did. So intent was his stare that Somerton found himself shaken from his trance only when a passerby loudly commanded, " 'Ere, step aside, out o' the way, if you've got to be gawking about all day!"

Immediately Darnell called across the crowded street, "Harriet! Miss Tremaine! Wait! I've got to talk with you!"

The figure did not pause but, with her back

to Somerton, continued along with a steady pace. Nevertheless, by the time Darnell had managed to cross the busy street, she had vanished. When it was borne in upon him that he had no hope of finding the woman he had seen, Darnell leaned against a storefront and tried to collect his thoughts. He was, he felt, going mad. Otherwise, how could one account for the outrageous manner in which he had behaved? To be sure, it was entirely possible that Miss Tremaine was in London. Even possible that she might be on this very street at the moment he passed. But she was, he reminded himself, only a governess. To call out in such a nonsensical manner, when he had not even seen her face, was absurd! And yet, Darnell was forced to admit to himself, it mattered very much to him that he thought he had seen Miss Tremaine. Slowly he recrossed the street and once more traced his steps homeward.

As for Miss Elisabeth Henrick, she stood in the shadows of a milliner's shop that looked directly out upon the street. Desperately she tried to calm herself. He had *not* found her! Indeed, he had gone away. There was no question in her mind, however, that she would not again wear these clothes. Her intended visit to Aunt Letty forgotten, Elisabeth's only wish was to return safely home.

"I doubt, miss, you can afford that hat," a clerk spoke from behind Miss Henrick.

Elisabeth turned to see the woman looking her up and down, not bothering to hide the contempt in her eyes. "What did you say?" Elisabeth asked politely.

The woman looked with meaning at a straw hat Elisabeth had absentmindedly picked up.

"I wouldn't crush that, miss," the woman said with a sniff, "for it wouldn't be within your means to pay for it, I'm sure."

Something stirred within Elisabeth. "Indeed?" she asked frostily. "I believe that is for me to decide." Without haste she removed her own bonnet and placed the straw creation on her head. "I'll take it," she said, after pretending to study her image in the looking-glass.

And so, a short time later, Miss Henrick left the milliner's shop, a neatly packed bandbox in hand. Elisabeth felt a trifle guilty at the unnecessary purchase and had to remind herself that she could now afford it. Regardless of how she looked, she was no longer a penniless governess. Governess. The near-encounter with Darnell Somerton, never entirely forgotten, once more flooded her thoughts, bringing colour to her cheeks. Elisabeth found herself dwelling less upon the terror of the experience than upon the fact of its occurrence. He had called out, "Harriet," first, and only then, "Miss Tremaine." Did he, could he still dwell upon that little brown wren he had known so briefly a year ago? Absurd, Elisabeth told herself sharply. And what is it to you if he does? Harriet Tremaine is gone. Forever. And neither you nor he shall ever see her again! For Elisabeth had determined to rid herself of Harriet Tremaine's clothes directly she returned home.

Nevertheless, for all her stern self-counsel, Elisabeth found her thoughts full of Mr. Darnell Somerton all the way home.

5

Almack's: it was a name that even after years of waiting could leave Elisabeth tremulous. No sensible reminder to herself of her twenty-four years could erase the fear caused by the knowledge that here she must present herself to Society and await the verdict. Here were to be found the *ton*'s strictest arbiters of propriety —the patronesses of Almack's. And no other credit meant so much as the entree to their select assemblies.

It was perhaps not surprising, therefore, that Elisabeth found no comfort in her mirror the night she was to make her first appearance at Almack's. To Marietta's critical eye it was otherwise. A dress of pale-green satin with open robe of lace matched Elisabeth's eyes perfectly. Brown curls clustered becomingly about her head and a dainty foot peeped from beneath the hem of the girl's dress. Elegant gloves straight from Paris and a simple strand of fine pearls completed the toilette.

"*Not* in your first blush of youth," Marietta pronounced frankly, "and it would be foolish to pretend otherwise. Nevertheless I do not despair, Elisabeth, of seeing you creditably established."

"In one night?" Elisabeth asked irrepressibly.

"Well, no," Marietta conceded, "but you must agree it is a start. Certainly no one will be able to find fault with your appearance, which is more than one can say of some of the girls we shall see there. One must be grateful for every advantage!"

"Shall we set it about that I am a great heiress?" Elisabeth asked, her eyes dancing. "Or is it grand passion I should be seeking?"

"Oh, do give over such nonsense at once," Marietta scolded with a sternness belied by the gleam in her own eyes. "Of course we shan't be so foolish as to expect great romance, for I have often observed that gentlemen only fall into such helpless passions with girls just out of the schoolroom. A most discouraging circumstance, I am sure, but one past mending. Nor," she added firmly, "shall we lie about your prospects."

Somewhat more seriously Elisabeth asked, a slight catch in her voice, "What sort of suitor do I look for, then?"

Marietta answered with the readiness of one who has given much thought to a matter. "Oh, I daresay we shall find any number of gentlemen, past the age of nonsense, who are casting about for someone to look after their comfort and provide them with excellent conversation."

Miss Henrick bit back a gurgle of laughter. A trifle unsteadily she said, "How . . . how old do . . . do you estimate such gentlemen will . . . will prove to be?"

Marietta, who was engrossed in coaxing a final curl of her own into place, offered offhandedly, "Oh, I warrant we may find a plentiful supply of such gentlemen still on this side of forty. And even, perhaps, one or two as young as thirty, though it would be best not to depend upon that."

It was, Elisabeth reflected ruefully, fortunate that she placed very little stock in Marietta's chatter. Otherwise, she would have found her spirits quite downcast at the future her cousin had laid out for her. To spend her life as the companion of a sober, older man seemed intolerable. Instead, her mind was full of visions of handsome young men, and however hopeless such dreams might be, Elisabeth clung to them. Or, at any rate, to one vision of one gentleman.

"Wool-gathering, my dear?" Marietta asked dryly, scattering Elisabeth's errant thoughts. "I should consider that an excellent sign, if it had occurred after the ball! As it is, we are keeping Hugh waiting and you must know that is something he detests. Come along and let us see what he has to say about your dress."

With a laugh, Elisabeth good-naturedly gathered her skirts and led the way downstairs. Halfway down she spied her cousin and called out gaily, "Well, Cousin Hugh? Shall I pass muster, do you suppose?"

Hugh Henrick was an amiable man and, when he paused to think about the matter, exceedingly fond of Elisabeth. She was, at times, a trifle sober for his tastes, but a few months of balls and routs and parties ought to fix that up, all right and tight. "Aye, that and more," he said aloud. "If, that is, anyone can keep their eyes off my Marietta."

"What faradiddles," his wife retorted with a laugh. She preened slightly and added, "I must say, however, I think this jonquil suits me very well, even if Mrs. Worthingham says that I am too old to wear such colours."

"Never," Elisabeth answered fondly.

"To the devil with such spiteful tabbies," Hugh contributed cheerfully.

"So long as you are contented," Marietta told her husband warmly, "then that is precisely where everyone else may consign their opinions! And now, let us go in to dinner."

"Aye, and then Almack's," he retorted soundly.

In deference to Marietta's wishes, the party reached Almack's neither among the first nor among the last arrivals. There were a sufficient number of people about that Marietta found no lack of opportunity to present Elisabeth to acquaintances, but not so many that she was instantly forgotten. And before they had been there scarcely ten minutes, Elisabeth had the satisfaction of having her hand solicited for a dance.

And yet it could not be denied that Miss Elisabeth Henrick did not take. The gentlemen found her conversation amiable and intelligent. More than one even pronounced her an exceedingly attractive young lady. But this was not enough, it seemed, to overcome the handicap of her age when there were so many younger girls to be met. Perhaps, had she indeed been an heiress, the matter might have been otherwise, but her mother's bequest was only a pleasant competence. Future evenings would, no doubt, prove less discouraging, but tonight not all of Marietta's efforts could prevent Elisabeth from joining the ranks of the wallflowers.

Incurably optimistic, Marietta took measure of the situation and said to Elisabeth, "Well, it is unfortunate, to be sure, but I do not despair. We shall seat ourselves over here and any gentleman wishing to enter the cardroom shall have to pass us by. Depend upon it, I am not yet ready to surrender. Smile, my dear, smile."

Elisabeth did more than smile. She laughed at her cousin's irrepressible determination. And, indeed, she did not find the evening so oversetting as another young woman might have. In this, her years as a governess stood her in good stead, for she had often had to smile and curtsey cheerfully when her spirits had been far from happy. Marietta's scheme did not, moreover, seem in the least foolish to Elisabeth. And, indeed, there were, from time to time, gentlemen who paused to greet Marietta and were then amiable enough to solicit a dance with her young cousin.

Upon returning to Marietta's side after one such dance and watching the gentlemen disappear into the cardroom, Elisabeth said dryly, "I begin to think, cousin, that we had best give out that I am an heiress, after all. I see no other remedy to save me from the dire fate of spinsterhood."

As Miss Henrick spoke, a gentleman nearby halted. He was impeccably dressed and moved with an air of decided assurance. It was Darnell Somerton. Directed by an impulse he could not name, Somerton lifted his quizzing-glass and surveyed the girl. The glass was an affectation, but a useful one in the event one was called upon to depress the pretensions of an overzealous matchmaker. The young lady who had spoken, he concluded, was of an age to be considered almost upon the shelf, however attractive she might be. A pity, particularly as her words indicated she had not even a fortune to aid her. But that was her problem. Somerton was about to turn away with a shrug when the girl raised her eyes and looked directly at him. Then the oddest thing occurred. She blushed fiercely, almost defiantly, it seemed, and quickly looked away. Before he quite realised what he was about, Darnell was at her side, bowing and saying, "May I present myself, Miss—?"

"Miss Henrick," Marietta supplied helpfully, "my cousin. Elisabeth, dear, this is Mr. Darnell Somerton."

"How . . . how do you do," she said faintly.

Not an auspicious beginning. And yet there was something about the girl that led Darnell to say, "Will you dance with me, Miss Henrick?"

Once more Elisabeth coloured. In a voice that was more brusque than she intended, Elisabeth said, "I cannot, Mr. Somerton. In spite of my years I am still in my first Season and have not yet received permission to waltz." At his blank expression she explained, a trifle impatiently, "It *is* a waltz they are playing. Hadn't you noticed?"

Darnell drew his brows together in something of a frown, an expression Elisabeth remembered only too well. "May I have the next dance, then, Miss Henrick?" he persisted.

Feeling hunted and more than a little desperate, Elisabeth showed fear on her face. After a moment Somerton straightened, his face a wooden mask. Marietta attempted to remedy matters. "Pray forgive my cousin, Mr. Somerton," she said earnestly. "I am sure you will understand that a girl in her first Season—"

Icily Somerton cut her short. "I understand, ma'am, that for some reason your cousin has taken a dislike, if not a fear, of me. While I cannot fathom the cause, I assure you I find the feeling quite mutual and have no intention of inflicting my presence upon her any longer."

With that, Somerton turned on his heel and crossed the room to speak with another young lady. Marietta could only turn to her cousin and moan weakly, "Oh, Elisabeth!"

Elisabeth had gone quite pale herself, and she spoke with some difficulty. "I . . . I am not feeling well, Marietta."

"The rooms are over there," Marietta said hastily with a wave of her hand. "Do you wish me to come with you?"

Elisabeth shook her head. She gathered her skirt in one hand and headed in the direction indicated, leaving Marietta with head held high, attempting to smile placidly. Even in Elisabeth's distressed state, however, it was impossible to be unaware that the scene with Mr. Somerton had been observed by a great many people. Had anything been wanted to set the seal on her fate as a wallflower, Elisabeth was well aware that this had done so. On impulse she changed her direction and headed for the door. In a quiet antechamber outside the ballroom, a note was quickly written and dispatched to her cousin. Hugh and Marietta would no doubt be appalled that she had fled Almack's, but she hoped they would understand.

Once outside, a hack was quickly procured by a footman, and a short time later Elisabeth was home. She stayed only long enough to change clothes. A friendly groom had, after her near-encounter with Darnell, been persuaded to loan her a set of clothes, and she slipped out the back door as soon as she had changed into them. Then, as she had tried to do the day before, she set forth for Letty's house.

Letty's butler had not seen the boy before, but he was persuaded to carry a note up to his mistress. To his surprise, La Perdita immediately directed that the boy be placed in the bookroom to await her. There, unaccountably, the boy refused the offer of a mug of ale and kept to himself. But then *some* people did take on airs above themselves!

Elisabeth had only a short time to wait before Letty swept into the room. Her first words were, "Good God!" Hastily Letitia shut the door behind her and advanced towards her niece, a frown upon her face. "Why are you here, my dear?" she asked, with concern. "And in such absurd clothes? It's a slow evening for me, I'll warrant you, but *you* should be at Almack's."

"I've just come from there," Elisabeth began.

"Dressed like that?" Letty demanded with the liveliest astonishment. "Surely Marietta would never have permitted such a thing? Why I would have heard if—"

What Letty would have heard Elisabeth was never to know, for she blurted out desperately, "I've ruined myself, Letty!"

For once Letitia was speechless and could only sink into the nearest chair as she stared blankly at her niece. Oddly, this steadied Elisabeth, who went on, "And not because I went dressed like this, to Almack's, for I did not. I was, I assure you, clad most properly, most demurely, in a green satin gown from Suzette."

"Then, how?" Letty asked, bewildered. "Did some gentleman offer you an insult?"

"The other way around, I'm afraid," Elisabeth replied wryly. "Mr. Darnell Somerton asked me to dance and I snubbed him."

At these words, Letitia sat upright and regarded her niece shrewdly. "That seems most unlike you. Did he recognise you?"

Elisabeth shook her head. "No, I am certain he did not. But I was quite afraid he had, which is why I was so foolish as to panic. I fear I must be the greatest pea goose alive!"

Letitia leaned back against the cushions of her chair. "I think you'd best begin at the start and tell me all about it," she commanded quietly.

Elisabeth stared at her hands, pleased to see they were no longer shaking. "Yesterday I started out to visit you, dressed as Harriet Tremaine. Somerton saw me and called out my—her name. I managed to evade him but could not bring myself to do other than return home. At once. Which is why," she said with a smile, "you see me dressed as a boy tonight. It seemed much the safest disguise." Letitia nodded and Elisabeth went on, "I tell you that so you will understand why, when I saw Mr. Somerton at Almack's tonight, I felt such fear. I could not believe he had not once again recognised me. And by the time I did realise it, I had already offended him." She paused and smiled ruefully. "My behaviour was abominable and he went away furious, and I, I fled—as discreetly as possible—here."

"For advice?" Elisabeth nodded and Letitia said, with admirable calm, "Quite right. Though I own I wish your cousin Marietta were not such a widgeon, for then it would not be necessary to put yourself at such risk."

"But what do I do?" Elisabeth leaned forward and demanded.

"That, my dear, depends upon what you wish the outcome to be." Letty smiled and counted the options off on her fingers. "You might, for example, simply wish to forget the matter and treat Mr. Somerton with indifferent civility when he next speaks to you, as I have no doubt he shall. Or you could simply flee and give up all hope of acceptance by the *ton*."

Letty paused and looked at Elisabeth, who said dryly, "Go on. I feel sure you have another alternative for me."

La Perdita smiled. "I do. Go after him! Politely, of course, and with all due regard for the proprieties. Apologise, but not by note. Do so in person. Tell him you had the headache. Anything! At a party or supper or ball the matter is easily arranged."

Letty snapped her fingers triumphantly, but Elisabeth was not so easily convinced. "I do not perceive how this helps me," she said bluntly.

"At your age, of course not," Letitia replied soothingly. "But for me the matter is clear. Mr. Somerton is intrigued. Perhaps it is something that reminds him of a certain governess. Perhaps not. But now you have snubbed him. He is not, believe me, sufficiently intrigued to persist unless you once more arouse his interest."

"How?" Elisabeth asked. "By being brazenly forward? Insulting him anew? I cannot believe either will answer. And if they did, what, then?"

"Why, then, the *ton* will see that so eligible a bachelor as Mr. Darnell Somerton shows an interest in Miss Elisabeth Henrick, and her success is assured!"

"And I court the risk of being unmasked by him," Elisabeth said quietly. "Yesterday he recognised me easily enough."

"You were dressed as Harriet Tremaine," Letitia pointed out calmly. "He did not know you face to face tonight." Abruptly she leaned forward and took her niece's hands in her own. "Elisabeth, you cannot live in a prison of fear. It is not for that we've worked so hard! In this life we risk far more by being timid than by being bold. Avoid Mr. Somerton and he will surely wonder why. Seek him out and he may soon tire of you. Certainly he will not suspect that you have something to hide from him. From what you have told me, Harriet Tremaine was a bold, outspoken creature, plain and yet arresting in her very uniqueness. But Miss Henrick, ah, she is all propriety and respectable conversation and even something of a beauty."

"Suppose . . ." Elisabeth paused and blushed furiously. "Suppose I cannot act the part convincingly? Or that he does not tire of me and . . . and develops a *tendre* for me?"

With mock sternness Letty cast an eye on her niece. "I think it must be vapid conversation and utter insipidness," she said firmly. "You know very well what sort of thing I mean, and will find it easier, I'll wager, than being a governess. As for Mr. Somerton," she stopped and sighed. "I might wish for the sake of your happiness that he would, but you must know he is accounted the most confirmed of bachelors! Boldness is one thing, but to try for the moon quite madness."

'Yes, Aunt Letty," Elisabeth replied meekly.

"Good. Now along with you. It will never do to have Marietta or Hugh discover you have been here," Letitia said firmly.

Obediently Elisabeth rose to her feet. "Very well. I shall dance to your tune," she said. "Anything must be preferable to inaction! Thank you, Aunt Letty."

Elisabeth started toward the door of the bookroom but Letty's voice halted her. "Be careful, my dear. I shouldn't wish you to get into any further trouble, on your way home."

Elisabeth only nodded. She had no intention of looking for trouble or allowing herself to be unmasked. In any event, she had too many other matters to dwell upon. Her boy's cap set firmly on her head, Elisabeth was let out by a footman, and a short time later she slipped through the Henricks' back door and up the rear staircase. The voices of Hugh and Marietta were quite audible to her as they deplored her heretofore unsuspected shyness. Perhaps there was the note to strike with Mr. Somerton! Oh, well, thought Elisabeth with a grin, Hugh and Marietta will no doubt be delighted by my behaviour when next I meet Darnell.

So it was with surprising ease that Elisabeth,

her groom's clothing safely stowed away, fell asleep that night. And if her dreams were all of a certain elegant gentleman, well, who was to know or care?

——6——

As with most of the *ton,* it was Marietta's custom to drive about the park each afternoon *if* the weather was delightful. And she was adamant that Elisabeth accompany her. "One never knows whom one may meet there or what invitations may be solicited," Marietta told her cousin firmly as she drew on her gloves the afternoon after Elisabeth's debacle at Almack's. "It was upon just such an occasion, you must know, that I was introduced to Hugh! We must make up our minds to arrange something equally fortunate for you. And after last night, if you do not appear with me, everyone will say it is because of your encounter with Mr. Somerton and *that* will be more of an *on-dit* than ever! Besides, you may encounter some of your old friends from school, and that can never hurt."

Elisabeth refrained from pointing out that more than six years of silence had cut what few school ties she had had. Still, Marietta's comments about her encounter with Darnell made sense, and in any case, she was too accustomed to Marietta's high-handedness to object. She contented herself with the cheerful reply, "I daresay. But with that new pelisse of yours, you are the one who shall have to fend off the admirers!"

Marietta laughed and looked down at herself with satisfaction. "To be sure, this shade of blue has always become me," she said. "But you are far more striking in the rose. I do believe Suzette was inspired in choosing it for you. Depend upon it, you shall be quite out of the common way!" Marietta paused as she realised that this was not, perhaps, the most felicitous of observations. Fixing Elisabeth with a stern eye, she added, "You will, I trust, be civil to everyone we may meet? Even if that should include Mr. Somerton? I declare I felt quite ready to sink last night! How unlike you to behave with such rudeness. I do wish you could explain it to me. Not," she said, holding up her hand, "that I wish to hear some tale about a *headache*. You have never suffered from such nonsense in your life."

As Marietta paused for breath, Elisabeth cheerfully cut her short. "I thought you said you were pledged to meet Lady Welton at the park. Oughtn't we to be going?"

"Oh, dear, yes!" Marietta exclaimed. "At once!"

Marietta need not have worried. It was such a fine day that the park was positively crowded with carriages, horses, and persons on foot. Not the most exacting of friends could have chided Mrs. Henrick for her delay. Predictably, Lady Welton had one of her daughters beside her, a girl who showed not the least desire to converse with Elisabeth. Indeed, the girl's reserve was so marked that Elisabeth found herself hoping something would occur to rescue her.

At the same moment, Olivia Somerton, her husband, and her brother-in-law were riding through the park on horseback. In good-humour she was roasting Darnell. "Who is this chit who refuses to swoon over you, Darry?" she asked with more than idle curiosity. "It is all very well for you to be given such a set-down, keeps you from becoming all puffed up in your own conceit, you know, but I should like to know what sort of girl could treat a Somerton with disdain."

Darnell, who had been listening with remarkable patience, said calmly, "Well, you may see for yourself, if you wish. She is over there, in the carriage next to Lady Welton's." He paused and added mischievously, "Shall I introduce you? Or is a look sufficient?"

Olivia, who was not noted for restraint, took up the challenge and said, with a laugh, "Oh, by all means, introduce us to this girl! If she is unbearable, why, then, we shall even the score by snubbing her soundly."

Darnell frowned, about to withdraw the offer. His sister-in-law, well aware of his intent, did not wait, but spurred her horse toward the two carriages. Darnell and Robert had no choice but to follow. Even so, they were almost too late. Olivia was forced, literally, to overtake Mrs. Henrick's carriage. A trifle breathlessly she called out, "Wait! I wish to speak with you!"

Out of pure astonishment, Marietta reined in her horses. "Me?" she said, blinking at the lady on horseback. "Are we acquainted?"

At that moment, Robert and Darnell reached the group, and Olivia lowered her eyes demurely. "Actually, I believe you are acquainted

with my brother-in-law. Darry, pray do introduce us!" she commanded in a low voice.

A trifle stiffly, Darnell did so. "Mrs. Henrick,
Miss Henrick, may I present my brother and
his wife?"

"Oh, don't be stuffy," Olivia said hastily.
"I'm Olivia and this is Robert."

Marietta seemed too dazed to reply and Elisabeth took matters into her own hands. "How
do you do?" she said with a friendly smile.
"I'm Elisabeth."

"And . . . and I am Marietta Henrick," her
cousin said faintly.

Olivia managed, no one quite knew how, to
maneuver the party so that Darnell found himself next to Miss Henrick while his sister-in-
law engaged Mrs. Henrick in conversation.
Rather grimly, Darnell considered wringing
Olivia's neck.

Abruptly Elisabeth captured his attention
by saying, in a voice that reached his ears
alone, "Mr. Somerton, I regret that I was so
rude yesterday."

"Quite all right, I assure you," he replied in
his most daunting manner. "It is not of the
slightest importance."

Something stirred within Elisabeth at the
haughtiness of this reply, and even without
Letty's instructions, she would have pushed
on recklessly. With a voice that must have
done credit to any actress upon the stage, she
said breathlessly, "Oh, sir, I can only plead a
shyness that overwhelms me at times!"

That caught his interest. Meeting her eyes,
he discovered that she had not entirely succeeded in suppressing their liveliness. Indeed,
they almost seemed to invite him to share a

secret jest. With no little asperity, Darnell told her, "Miss Henrick, there is not the least trace of shyness in your manner!"

She lowered her eyes and said with a mournful sigh, "Alas, I know it, sir! And that is what makes it all the more distressing when such attacks do occur."

To his surprise, Somerton realised that whatever dislike he had felt for Miss Henrick the night before was swiftly being replaced by a sense of amused kinship. Entering into the spirit of things, he said gravely, "It must be a terrible cross to bear, Miss Henrick. Have you tried parsley tea? I understand it to perform wonders in curing such disorders!"

"Par . . . parsley tea?" Elisabeth demanded, biting her lip to keep from laughing outright. "You are, sir, outrageous."

Before he could reply, Olivia turned her attention to Elisabeth and said, "Miss Henrick! I understand this to be your first Season, and I find myself at a loss to understand why."

The laughter left Elisabeth's eyes, a circumstance which did not escape Darnell's attention. Rather quietly Miss Henrick answered, "Yes, this is. My mother was ill for many years and I am afraid a Season was out of the question."

Which was, she reflected silently, the truth. Undaunted, Mrs. Somerton persisted, "Are you enjoying your Season?"

Again Elisabeth's answer held a great deal of truth as she said, "Very much, Mrs. Somerton. It is a delightful change from what I have been accustomed to!"

Olivia looked sideways at her brother-in-law. Lowering her lashes, she said provocatively,

"What a pity you and Darnell have taken each other in such dislike."

With impeccable *sang-froid* Darnell replied, "You are mistaken, Olivia, we have not." He looked down at Elisabeth's face, which had gone pale, and smiled reassuringly. "Indeed, it was all a misunderstanding; Miss Henrick and I are now upon the best of terms."

"Indeed?" Olivia said skeptically.

Marietta, who looked about to faint, murmured, "How . . . how fortunate."

Robert, goaded finally by his wife's behaviour, snapped at her, "Really, Olivia! What do you expect him to say?"

Darnell flicked a graceful finger at an imaginary speck of dust on the sleeve of his riding coat. "I do wish," he drawled, "that both of you would cease to take such an interest in my affairs. Indeed, I wish you will both go away and allow me to speak with Miss Henrick in peace."

He raised his eyes to look at them, and Robert and Olivia hastily withdrew. While generally the most amiable of brothers, he possessed, they knew, a streak of sternness that made it unwise to push him too far. Darnell watched them go, then turned once more to Elisabeth. "My apologies," he said with a quiet smile that was oddly reassuring.

Elisabeth could only smile in return, but Marietta gushed, "So kind, Mr. Somerton! And so kind of Mrs. Somerton to condescend to speak to us! I am sure it is no wonder she was puzzled by Elisabeth's behaviour last night. I declare, it is most kind of you to overlook it!"

Smoothly Mr. Somerton cut her short. "But I have *not* overlooked it," he said with faint surprise. "Indeed, it is expressly with that point in mind that I am about to ask Miss Henrick to go out driving with me tomorrow," he said. Then, fixing her with a mock-stern stare he added, "You do not dare refuse me this time, Miss Henrick, for I should never forgive you if you did. Besides, it will help you get over your attacks of shyness!"

Entering into the spirit of things, Elisabeth replied with a twinkle in her eyes, "I should never be so cruel as to cut you two days in a row, Mr. Somerton! At what hour shall we drive out?"

"At what hour will you find yourself least shy?" he countered.

With a laugh she named a time, and matters were quickly arranged. Somerton took his leave a few minutes later.

Marietta was, it seemed, overcome with delight at this unexpected good fortune and could not refrain from telling her cousin, over and over again, how auspicious this all was. Elisabeth, however, was beginning to feel worried. She was, it was true, following Letty's advice, but somehow matters seemed to be getting out of hand. Letty had meant all this to lead merely to a light flirtation, and instead, Elisabeth knew with a sinking sensation, it was already too late. For whatever absurd reason, her heart was already tied up with Somerton's.

So intent was Elisabeth on her thoughts that she did not even see the lovely Duchess of Carston observing her from a carriage not very far away. Even if she had, it is unlikely she would have cared. For even with the sinking feeling inside, Elisabeth was conscious of a growing sense of elation. Whatever the future, tomorrow she was pledged to go out driving with Mr. Darnell Somerton!

7

Had it been possible, Darnell Somerton would have cried off from the engagement to go out driving. More than one friend had expressed astonishment that he deigned to notice Miss Henrick at all, and Darnell had the uncomfortable feeling that his interest in her was likely to subject him to any number of such comments. Miss Henrick, it is true, was something of a beauty. But after years of pronounced avoidance of the *ton*'s most eligible girls, nothing less than a diamond of the first water would be expected to capture his attention. Nothing would have been simpler, of course, than to concoct an excuse and send it round in a note to her. Had she been a featherbrained chit, it might have been possible to do so. Unfortunately, she was not, and that was part of the reason Darnell found himself attracted to her in the first place. He was also unhappily aware that if he broke his promise to take her out driving, the universal opinion would be that for some obscure reason Darnell had been trifling with Miss Henrick. The *ton* did not approve of such behaviour. More important, Darnell Somerton did not approve. It was no part of his nature to alternately raise a girl's hopes and then dash them. Nor could he be certain that his inner

devil would not prompt him to single out Miss
Henrick again when next he saw her, for the
very reason he wished to cancel the appointed
drive was that he felt far too attracted to Miss
Henrick for his own comfort. And he was not
at all sure that he wished to feel this way
about any woman. Perhaps the hurt that Pamela had married the duke in preference to
him was still too strong. Perhaps it was that
he had simply grown accustomed to light
flirtations. Either way, Darnell felt himself
more nervous for this one drive than he could
recall feeling in the past ten years.

Had he but known it, Miss Henrick shared
Somerton's reservations. As she dressed in her
favourite walking dress of green with its lace
fichu at the throat, Elisabeth could not refrain
from voicing her concern to Marietta. "Perhaps
I ought to cry off," she said timidly.

"My love, you cannot," Marietta said, going
pale. "To refuse Mr. Somerton's invitation now
would be unthinkable! Depend upon it, everyone would say you had deliberately snubbed
him. And without the slightest excuse. And it
would be true! I cannot, even with my fondness for you, Elisabeth, begin to understand
why a nonpareil such as Mr. Somerton has
chosen to show such a gratifying interest in
you. But there can be no reason, save prejudice,
for you to snub him!"

Elisabeth turned away and pretended to fix
a curl. Impossible to explain, for Marietta knew
nothing of the existence of Harriet Tremaine.
Nor could she explain that she was afraid of
being hurt, afraid that Darnell was only amused
at her while she . . . she cared far too much.
After a moment, however, she turned back to

her cousin and smiled reassuringly. "You needn't worry, Marietta. I promise I shan't disgrace myself today. Indeed, I shall be all that is amiable towards Mr. Somerton."

Marietta Henrick did not trouble to hide her sigh of relief. Elisabeth was a good girl, but there was no denying she had an odd kick in her gallop, as Hugh was wont to say. But Mrs. Henrick was an amiable woman and she held her tongue, merely seeing to it that Elisabeth did not keep Mr. Somerton waiting above five minutes. And that was surely no more than the gentleman expected!

Marietta was quite correct. Indeed, Mr. Somerton was agreeably surprised by Miss Henrick's relative promptness. He had, he realised, more than half-expected her to snub him. As for Mrs. Henrick, she was all flattering attention. "*Such* a fine day, Mr. Somerton! I've no doubt you are impatient to be going. You cannot wish to keep your horses standing on such a brisk day, particularly such high-spirited horses as I presume them to be."

Somerton bowed politely. So tautly were his nerves stretched that he said, rather shortly, "If Miss Henrick is ready?"

A gleam appeared in Elisabeth's eyes and she curtseyed, simpering, "Of course, Mr. Somerton. Though I do hope your horses are not *too* spirited. I should be frightened half to death, if they are!"

An answering smile appeared in Darnell's eyes as he rather sheepishly relaxed. Before he could apologise for his abruptness, however, Marietta had been moved to protest. "Why, Elisabeth Henrick! I have it on excellent authority that you have never been afraid of a horse in your life! What is this nonsense? I do hope you are not going to be missish. *That* would be unforgivable!''

Darnell Somerton shot a swift, shrewd look at Miss Henrick. He bowed to her, then said to Marietta, ''Why, I shall do my best, Mrs. Henrick, to set your cousin at her ease. You are quite right to take me to task for being so abrupt with her.''

Marietta felt as though the ground were shifting directly under her feet. She was too astonished to do more than blink and open and shut her mouth. Darnell seized the opportunity to hold out a hand to Elisabeth. ''Shall we be going, Miss Henrick? I promise that you shall not find me an ogre and that I shall keep a firm hand on my horses.''

There was a gentle warmth about his smile that removed the outrageousness from his speech. Not trusting herself to reply, however, Elisabeth nodded and took his hand. Neither said very much, in fact, until they were seated in Mr. Somerton's phaeton and he had given the order for his groom to stand away from the horses' heads. Then, in absolute disregard of convention, Darnell drove away without waiting for the poor fellow to take up his place behind them.

Her voice a trifle unsteady, Elisabeth said, ''How . . . how original of you.''

The barest trace of a smile crossed Somerton's face as he replied, ''Do you mind? I had the oddest impression, you know, that in the matter of eccentricity, Miss Henrick, you and I were well-matched.'' He paused and then said seriously, ''If you are truly distressed, I shall return for my groom, but I thought both you and I would be grateful for the freedom to speak as we wished rather than as the rest of society regards as proper."

Elisabeth could only be thankful that the penetrating gaze he turned on her lasted only a moment. She judged it wisest not to answer him directly but instead to say, "I enjoyed meeting your sister-in-law yesterday, Mr. Somerton."

"Did you? How splendid for you."

Elisabeth tried again. "The weather seems surprisingly mild for this time of year."

"Does it? How splendid for you."

Elisabeth's eyes narrowed and her voice was a trifle tart as she said, "I think you must take great pride in your horses, sir, for you honour them with so much attention."

"Do you think so? How—"

"*Splendid for you!*" Elisabeth said through clenched teeth.

Darnell grinned appreciatively, and after a moment her anger dissolved into laughter.

"*Do* you possess any other conversation?" she demanded tartly.

It was Somerton's turn to ignore the question. By now they had reached the park and he turned his attention to the matter of guiding his horses through the gateway. Only then did he turn to Elisabeth and say, with unexpected friendliness, "That's much better. I cannot, in general, abide insipidness. Will you tell me why you must pretend to it?"

To her astonishment, Elisabeth felt her eyes begin to fill with tears. She sniffed resolutely and said coolly, "Perhaps you are mistaken, Mr. Somerton. Perhaps I merely lack town bronze and am indeed this curious mixture of insipidness and forwardness you see."

"Impossible!" he retorted bluntly. His eyes danced as he went on, "You laugh too easily and I like you far too well for that to be true. Which must be the most absurd thing I have ever said, for I can't possibly know you well enough to say such things at all."

Elisabeth's eyes flew up to meet his and fell just as swiftly. "Of . . . of course," she agreed faintly.

Somerton was in no hurry to answer. When he did, he said dryly, "I do wonder, you know, why you are in such a panic with me, at times. Have you something to hide? A squint, perhaps? A family skeleton? I have it! A mad desire to run away to sea?"

Elisabeth could not help laughing. It was with some spirit that she retorted, "Now, that is truly absurd! And you are the most . . . most complete hand I have ever met. I take leave to tell you, sir, that your view of yourself is highly inflated if you believe I care so very much what you think."

It was a desperate measure and Somerton's response was no more than she expected. "Good! Then I needn't hesitate to tell you, Miss Henrick, that you are the most exasperating female I have ever encountered. Furthermore, you are in strong need of a husband to take you in hand and teach you some manners!"

As Somerton glared at her, Elisabeth started to laugh. "My cousin Marietta is of precisely the same opinion," she told him frankly. "And I assure you she is doing her best to fulfill the prescription. Unfortunately there don't seem to be a great many gentlemen who aspire to fill the role, and I doubt there are any who could."

Darnell Somerton was about to reply in kind when it occurred to him that to do so might lead to waters over his head. Forcing his tone to a lightness he did not feel, Darnell replied coolly, "I shall be curious to see if you are right, Miss Henrick. Tell me, what do you think of the theatre this year? I find Kean somewhat past his prime."

Elisabeth looked at the stiff profile beside her and said, in her most daunting voice, "Do you? How splendid for you." Somerton's pretense dissolved in uncontrollable laughter as Elisabeth watched. "You deserved that, you know," she told him amiably.

"So I did," Darnell agreed. He placed one hand over hers. "Shall we call a truce? I should greatly dislike wasting our acquaintance on such nonsense."

Elisabeth smiled sunnily at her companion, a mischievous glint to her eyes. "Certainly, Mr. Somerton. I have the greatest wish to be on good terms with you, you know."

"Why?" he asked suspiciously.

A gurgle of laughter escaped her. "Because it will do my credit any amount of good to be seen in amiable conversation with you, of course."

Her eyes invited him to share the jest, and Somerton found that he did. "Well, that puts me in my place, doesn't it?" he said with a smile.

Before either could think of anything more outrageous to say, a soft voice called to them, "Darry! Oh, Darry, do pull up and let me talk with you."

From the expression on Somerton's face, it was evident that he did not altogether wish to do so. Nevertheless, he obediently brought his phaeton to a halt. With a polite expression he watched as the lady on horseback approached. She was flanked, as usual, Elisabeth felt sure, by several handsome gentlemen. All of whom the lady waved away when she reached Somerton's carriage.

"Hello, Pamela," Darnell said when she was close enough. "What do you wish to say to me?"

Pamela pouted charmingly. "Why, Darry, I only wished to meet your pretty companion."

"Miss Henrick, may I present the Duchess of Carston? Pamela, may I present Miss Elisabeth Henrick?"

For Elisabeth there was a sense of *déjà-vu* in all this. She felt, also, a trace of fear that the duchess might recognise her. She need not have worried. Pamela was far too concerned with Darnell to look closely at his companion. Indeed, she looked directly at Somerton, ignoring the harshness in his voice as she said, with some surprise, "Miss *Henrick*? Why, surely I recall some little *contretemps* . . . ?"

Without the least trace of a smile Somerton replied wearily, "Really, your Grace! Must you listen to such gossip?"

Once more the duchess pouted. "I've provoked you, Darry. But I swear I meant no offence!" She paused and turned to Elisabeth. "He only calls me 'your Grace' when he is angry with me. But you understand, don't you, Miss Henrick? One can't help being fascinated by everything about Darry. Or can one? Whatever he may say, word has it that you were most unfascinated with him just a few days ago."

Pamela paused and regarded Elisabeth from under delicately arched brows. Somerton would have intervened, but Elisabeth forestalled him. In the rather breathless manner he had heard her use the day before, Elisabeth replied, "On the contrary, your Grace! 'Twas shyness I suffered, not a lack of fascination. Mr. Somerton has been most kind about the whole matter."

"Indeed?" the duchess said frostily. "How very odd."

"Her Grace does not suffer from your affliction," Darnell explained to Elisabeth politely.

Once more Elisabeth turned wide eyes to the duchess and said, breathlessly, "Oh, your Grace, I hope that by the time I reach your age, I shall have outgrown such attacks, as well!"

Pamela's eyes narrowed and glinted with anger. With great effort, she forced herself to smile. Gracefully she laid a possessive hand on Darnell's arm and said, "You haven't much time, then, my dear. And however much the gentleman my Darry can be, there is a limit to his patience."

Gently but firmly Darnell removed the gloved hand from his arm. Blandly he said, "Tell me, Pamela. How is the duke? I understood him to be suffering from the gout. Surely you should be at his bedside?"

The Duchess of Carston laughed and tossed her head. "He don't want me there," she retorted frankly. "Said he would rather think of me in London enjoying myself."

From his seated position in the phaeton,

Somerton managed a slight bow. "My felici-
tations, your Grace, upon having such an amiable husband. I trust you are suitably grateful
for your good fortune?"

This last was a question, one which Pamela
answered rather tartly. "I am suitably grateful
for my foresight in choosing such a husband.
But enough, Darry! We are putting poor Miss
Henrick to the blush." She looked directly at
Elisabeth, who did not deign to answer. Then,
abruptly, Pamela's expression altered. "Do you
know," she said in a puzzled voice, "I have the
oddest notion I've met you somewhere before."

The colour rose in Elisabeth's cheeks, but
she managed to reply with an entirely steady
voice, "Indeed, your Grace? I think it most
unlikely, for I am quite certain I would have
remembered you."

The duchess stared for a moment longer,
then shrugged. "No matter. I trust we shall
meet again." She paused and turned to Darnell,
but there was no welcome in his eyes. With a
cheerfulness she was far from feeling, she said,
"Well, my dear, I must be off. Don't forget
you are promised to attend my ball next week,
Darry! Good day, Miss Henrick."

Both Darnell and Elisabeth murmured some
sort of conventional remark and watched her
go. Only when she was out of earshot did
Somerton turn to Elisabeth and say, with some
asperity, "That was the most outrageous per-
formance I have ever seen, Miss Henrick."

She looked at him and said, seriously, "Are
you offended? I had the notion you were not
very pleased with her yourself."

"And what has that to say to the matter?"
he demanded.

"Nothing," Elisabeth admitted with an engaging grin, "save that I felt she deserved a set-down."

With mock gravity Somerton shook his head and said, "Miss Henrick, I fear for your future unless you are able to control this streak of levity that appears to be a part of you."

"But you are not offended?" she asked, a trifle anxiously.

"No, I am not offended," he agreed.

"Good!" Elisabeth said with a loud sigh of relief. She hesitated, then added, "You know, Mr. Somerton, if that is the sort of female you are acquainted with, it is no wonder you have shied clear of marriage."

"Miss Henrick!"

Elisabeth laughed. "I know. It is too bad of me to roast you like that. But I cannot otherwise account for your apparent dislike of my sex."

"And what do you know of my opinion of your sex?" he demanded frostily.

"Nothing, really," she said, turning disarmingly wide eyes on his. "But one cannot help but hear that Mr. Darnell Somerton is considered to be unlikely ever to wed. Oh, there is gossip that he is fond of certain *ineligible* females, or that he has had an interest, here or there, in ladies of the *ton*, but never an announcement in the papers."

"And you find that odd?" he asked haughtily.

"Yes, I do," Elisabeth replied frankly. "For you possess considerable address and features that women find very attractive. You are, moreover, past the age of reckless escapades and hey-go-mad pranks, so it is not a loss of freedom you fear. Particularly as I assure you

every young lady is well informed that one's
husband may have an interest in the muslin
set, even after marriage, and one is not to chide
him for it."

Curiosity warred with anger at her imper-
tinence, and finally Darnell said, quietly,
"You are a most unusual young woman, Miss
Henrick."

Elisabeth grimaced expressively. "So my cousins Hugh and Marietta are forever telling me.
They, I can tell you, are not altogether pleased."

Somerton could not entirely repress a smile
as he said, "I can well imagine they are not."
He paused, then said coolly, "While we are
speaking frankly, Miss Henrick, I should like
to ask *you* how it was that I had offended you.
I cannot recollect that we have met before this
Season, and yet I would swear you already
held me in dislike or distrust when I approached you at Almack's." Somerton paused
again, but before Elisabeth could concoct an
answer, he went on, in the same conversa-
tional tone, "It may have been mere prejudice,
of course, for you seem to have heard a great
deal of nonsense spoken, but even so, I should
like to know the source of that prejudice."

Elisabeth could only stammer, "I-I . . . You
are mistaken, sir."

Darnell regarded her mockingly. "So, your
frankness extends only to others, Miss Henrick.
Well, I thought you would not oblige me in
this and I am sorry for it. I shall take you home
now, Miss Henrick. It has been a most unusual
excursion."

He said very little as he guided his horses
through the London streets, and Elisabeth found
herself afraid to break the silence. As he drew

to a halt outside Hugh's townhouse, Somerton's groom came running forward, for he had, of course, been waiting there the whole time. At this point Darnell turned to Elisabeth and said coolly, "You will forgive me, Miss Henrick, for not accompanying you inside. I have other, er, pressing engagements."

Not trusting herself to speak, Elisabeth nodded and, with as much grace as she could muster, climbed down from the phaeton. Instantly the carriage pulled away from the curb.

Inside, Marietta was waiting to pounce on her. "Well, Elisabeth? Will Mr. Somerton be calling again? Did he seem taken with you? Were you seen by anyone we know?"

To these and the rest of her cousin's questions Elisabeth could only reply, rather blankly, "I don't know."

As soon as she was able, Elisabeth escaped to her room, pleading a slight headache, not caring how plausible that might seem. There she stared out the window, berating herself for her wretched tongue. Her sense of loss was greatest, perhaps, because she had almost begun to feel that here was a man she might someday tell about her past and he would not hold it against her.

8

Elisabeth need not have worried. It was not to be expected that Mr. Somerton would easily let go of such a mystery as Miss Henrick. And he did not. For several weeks she found herself the object of his attention, a circumstance Marietta found very gratifying. It was not so simple for Elisabeth. Each time she saw Darnell, she found herself more drawn to him, more eager to hear his voice. More than once she almost told him about her past and then drew back. It was madness, she knew, to believe this could all lead to marriage, everyone told her so. But good sense, she found, could not over-rule her heart.

It was a further irony, of course, that as Mr. Somerton's attentions grew more particular, the rest of the *ton* discovered Miss Henrick to be quite charming. An original, of course, but utterly charming *in spite of her age*. And so Elisabeth soon found herself surrounded by a court of admirers. It was a heady experience for her to never lack for supper partners or invitations to dance or for drives in the park. Elisabeth's old school friends, moreover, redis-covered her and took great delight in advising her which of her suitors to favour. All safely married themselves, it had been some time since they had enjoyed such sport. Unfortunately, Elisabeth reflected wryly, her friends called it folly to waste one's daydreams on Somerton. Indeed, Melanie had put the matter quite bluntly, "Darnell Somerton has been indifferent to every beauty of the past ten Seasons! He flirts, but no more than that. And as flattering as it may be to have him dance attendance on you, Lizzy, I should be remiss if I did not warn you that it can only be a game! Indeed, there are those who say it is because you once snubbed him and he intends some sort of revenge. Still, to have engaged his interest this long is no little thing!"

And so, despite her heart, Elisabeth treated Darnell with a certain wariness, tried to keep a certain distance. It was not easy. She found it hard to believe, when he spoke with her or laughed or shared some private thought, that it was all a game. Surely it meant more?

The Viscount Langston, hearing secondhand from friends about Darnell's latest flirtation, was inclined to agree with Melanie. And yet, no one knew better how unlike the boy it was to display such persistent attention for so long. On the other hand, he was disturbed by other rumours to the effect that Darnell had not cut his amorous connection with the Duchess of Carston. So it was that the viscount and his wife arrived in London, at the height of the Season, claiming "social obligations."

Darnell was not in the least deceived. Nor was he surprised when his father immediately asked to speak with him in the library. He led the way and, once there, carefully pulled the library doors closed after them. "What is it, sir?" he asked politely.

"Sit down," the viscount replied curtly. He remained standing. "I shall be frank with you, Darnell, for I prefer pound dealings. Word has reached me of your activities in regard to two ladies, and I should like to know whether there is any truth to these rumours."

He paused and Darnell took the opportunity to say, very politely, "And if I tell you this is not your affair?"

The viscount fixed his son with a withering stare. "Anything which touches on family honour is my affair."

Darnell sat upright, drawing his brows together in a puzzled frown, and said, "Perhaps you had best tell me what rumours you mean, sir. I had not thought my actions did touch on family honour."

The viscount gripped the back of a chair and met his son's eyes squarely. Very deliberately he said, "The Duke of Carston is an old friend and I do not propose to stand by and see him cuckolded by a son of mine!"

Darnell considered this reply for several moments before he answered, conversationally, "I wonder if I ought to tell you to go to the devil?"

To his credit, the viscount chuckled. "Aye, always the fire-eater, ain't you? But look here. If it were some bit of muslin you'd gotten involved with, I wouldn't say a word. But it ain't. No, nor some discreet love affair, either, for I'll be damned if that she-cat cares about anyone but herself. If you are involved, I shall be doubting your good sense."

For a very long moment Darnell was silent. When he spoke, it was gravely. "I have ceased to be infatuated with her Grace from the day she told me that she was marrying the duke and that it was solely because of the title and fortune he could offer her. I am surprised, however, that gossip still ties my name with hers. It is only, I assure you, because I have too much self-respect to be rude to her when we meet."

"Aye, that's as well, then," the viscount said grudgingly. "And this other female? A Miss Henrick? Ain't trifling with her, are you? Heard she snubbed you. Don't seem like you to take up with her after that."

Darnell regarded his father mildly. "I have a very great affection for you, sir, but for you to be saying these things is the outside of enough!"

Irritably the viscount retorted, "Ain't I allowed to take an interest in the females my son does? What sort of girl is she? Pretty? Featherbrained or a bluestocking? Dull or lively?"

With a sigh Darnell said, "May I remind you, Father, that you said yourself you weren't obliged to like my choice of bride?"

Startled, the viscount exclaimed, "So it's that way, is it? Asked her yet?"

"No."

"I see. Well, I *ain't* obliged to like her, but you'll recollect I said I was obliged to approve of her." Langston glared at his son. "When shall I meet her?"

"Today? For tea?" Darnell suggested politely.

It was the viscount's turn to stare in long silence. "So you're that sure of the girl," he said at last.

"I am," Darnell agreed quietly.

"Very well. Tea, then, today."

With marvellous grace, Darnell Somerton rose to his feet, bowed to his father, and withdrew

from the library. The note he wrote to Miss
Henrick a short time later, revealed none of
the trepidation he felt.

Dear Miss Henrick,
   Will you do me the honour of coming to
tea this afternoon at four o'clock? Lord
and Lady Langston would like very much
to meet you.
                              Respectfully,
                              Darnell Somerton

   The invitation ought, of course, to have come
from Lady Langston, but Darnell did not care
about such niceties. His note was quickly dispatched and the reply that came back did nothing to cause Darnell to think Miss Henrick had
been offended. He would have been surprised,
in fact, to learn that his note had caused the
lady a high degree of consternation.
   Precisely at four o'clock, the knocker sounded
and Philip announced the caller. "Miss Elisabeth Henrick."
   To an onlooker, it would have seemed as
though time froze while Elisabeth paused in
the doorway of the drawing-room. The viscount and his wife saw a young woman of
about twenty-four who seemed to have an
extraordinary degree of poise. Her face was
dominated by fine green eyes, framed by hair
becomingly arranged, and might well have been
called beautiful. Her shoes, gloves, and dress,
moreover, were of excellent quality, with an
elegant simplicity that proclaimed the wearer
to be a young woman of impeccable taste. Nor
did the viscount and his wife fail to see how
the girl's eyes softened when they chanced to
meet Darnell's.

As for Elisabeth, she saw first Darnell, then his parents. Neither Robert Somerton nor his wife, Olivia, were in evidence. Darnell was, she thought, intolerably masculine in his tightly fitted pantaloons and a jacket that seemed molded to his shoulders. He came forward and took her hand. "Miss Henrick, may I present my parents? Viscount and Lady Langston."

No trace of Elisabeth's inner confusion showed on her face as she curtseyed gravely. A lesser woman might have quailed at the stern and distant expression on Lord Langston's face. Elisabeth did not. Instead, she took heart at the welcoming smile Lady Langston gave her. "Come and sit by me," that redoubtable lady said kindly. "Your father is John Henrick, is he not? And your mother's name is Jennifer, I believe?"

Taking the chair indicated, she nodded. "Was," Eliabeth corrected her gently. "My mother died a little over a year ago. But yes, my father's name is John Henrick."

Lady Langston did not answer at once. Instead, she waited as the maid brought in the tea. Elisabeth had a moment to steal a glance at Darnell, who was, she thought, remarkably quiet. He and his father seemed to be staring at her, something Elisabeth could not altogether like. Indeed, it was almost a relief when Lady Langston once more turned her attention to Elisabeth and said, "Yes, I had heard. How is your father?"

Elisabeth coloured. "I . . . I don't know. It is so rare that I see him, you understand."

"How fortunate for you," the viscount's voice intruded bluntly. "I've never liked the fellow very much. As for your mother, I recall her as something of a timid mouse. You haven't much the look of either of them, you know."

Anger steadied Elisabeth as she replied, "Nevertheless, they are my parents and I do not care to hear them spoken of in such a manner."

To Elisabeth's surprise, the viscount laughed. "*Not* a timid mouse at all," he said decisively. "And I'll wager you've more character than either of them as well! No, no, I shan't come to cuffs with you, my dear. I don't care in the least about your parents, but I am curious as to why you were not brought out years ago. Or were you?"

"My mother was . . . was ill for some time," Elisabeth answered quietly the now-familiar query. "A Season was out of the question."

Before the viscount could speak again, Lady Langston did so. "Do you know, I have the most extraordinary notion that I have seen you somewhere before—somewhere totally unsuited to a Henrick?"

With a sinking sensation, Elisabeth realised that it was entirely possible. Her first employer had been quite fond of having Miss Tremaine bring her charges in to see company. Silently Elisabeth damned her Ladyship's sharp eyes. Aloud, however, she could only say, faintly, "Indeed, ma'am? How . . . how odd."

"Odd and most provoking," her Ladyship agreed, "for I can't recall where it was. I daresay it was someone with a great look of you. Still, you do have most unusual features."

With an audacity that frightened her, and a distaste for the need to lie, Elisabeth lowered her eyes and said, "Perhaps, Lady Langston, you saw one of . . . of my father's. . . . That is, he is said to have a number of ... of love children scattered about London and our home countryside."

If Lady Langston was silenced, his Lordship was not. "Love children!" he snorted. "I should rather have called them common bastards, for I cannot believe your father cares one whit about them or has ever troubled to make provision for any of them. Shabby, very shabby. And utterly unlike your grandfather in that respect."

"In your grandfather's day," Lady Langston added quietly, "gentlemen respected their responsibilities. But you are probably right. No doubt the girl I saw was some poor child, born the wrong side of the blanket, who managed to make her way to some respectable position somewhere. Well, whoever she may be, I wish the girl luck. I have never thought it fair that you and I and everyone else in the *ton* should be so fortunate merely by an accident of birth while others suffer dreadfully."

At this point, for the first time, Darnell spoke. "I should explain, Miss Henrick, that my mother makes it her business to try to do something about such suffering. She is forever going into slums or hospitals or supporting schools."

"No doubt you think me mad, or at the very least quite eccentric," Lady Langston told Elisabeth without the smallest trace of apology or embarrassment in her voice.

In spite of herself, Elisabeth was moved to say, "I do not think you mad, Lady Langston. I, too, have had reason to venture into slums and know very well the work that needs to be done there. But you are mistaken to believe that birth and wealth insulate—protect—us from suffering."

"You speak as though you have reason to know," Lady Langston said with raised eyebrows. "How extraordinary! You are quite out of the common way, my girl and you will either continue to be a smashing success or end an appallingly neglected wallflower. I shall be interested to see which it is."

Elisabeth had no answer. Darnell did, however. "I cannot think the matter in doubt," he said dryly.

There was a meaning in his voice that Elisabeth dared not believe in. Her colour rose, nor was it eased by the viscount's next words. "Well, she ain't a namby-pamby miss, Darnell, I'll say that for her. And you needn't look at me like that, Miss Henrick. You'll soon become accustomed to the notion that we detest roundaboutation here! Why, I wager your tongue will soon be a match for any of ours."

Elisabeth's eyes flew to Darnell's and he smiled reassuringly at her. She set down her teacup with a hand that was not altogether steady, and Darnell immediately said, "Well, enough of this. You have met Miss Henrick and she has met you. I don't doubt that she is now in need of fresh air. Miss Henrick, would you care for a turn in the park?"

Rather helplessly Elisabeth looked at her hostess, who smiled kindly and patted her hand. "Go ahead, my dear. The air will do you good."

"Indeed it will," the viscount said, seconding the notion. "Darnell, I presume you will wish to speak with me later?"

Feeling rather as though she were escaping from Bedlam, Elisabeth took her leave of the elder couple and allowed Darnell to lead her to the foyer. As his carriage and horses were brought round, he helped her on with her pelisse. "I've no doubt we shall have the park to ourselves, at this hour, for everyone else will be at their tea," Darnell told her with satisfaction. Elisabeth gave him a long look. Aware of this, he laughed and said, "Afraid I have windmills in my head, Miss Henrick?"

"Something of the sort," she agreed dryly.

"Well, perhaps I do," he retorted cheerfully. "Ah, here is my phaeton now," he said, and led her through the door the footman was holding open. That poor fellow was left with his own astonished conjectures.

For once, Darnell did not dismiss his groom, and Elisabeth leaned back against the cushions thoughtfully. As the moments passed, a smile began to turn up the corners of her mouth. She was too honest not to admit to herself that she was enjoying Darnell's madness, if madness it was. "You are," she said aloud, "the most complete hand! You have succeeded in planting me a facer, you know."

"And you, Miss Henrick, are remarkably well-acquainted with cant terms for a young lady. Particularly one who grew up in a household without brothers," he informed her amiably.

Elisabeth's eyes twinkled. It was scarcely possible, however, to explain that her knowledge came from the boys in the households in which she had been a governess. Or that she had been a prime favourite among them. Instead, she said airily, "Oh, one's friends often have brothers."

"To be sure," Darnell agreed dryly, "though

I cannot recall taking any great interest in *my* sisters' friends *or* speaking cant to them."

"Ah, but you were an older brother," Elisabeth riposted neatly. "Younger brothers are far more forthcoming."

"Are they, indeed?" Darnell asked cheerfully. "I wonder. I also wonder, Miss Henrick, if you have ever taken up fencing. I feel certain you would make a formidable opponent."

Elisabeth laughed. "You know," she said confidingly, "there are times when I like you very much indeed!"

"Are there?" he asked with a sudden, intense warmth.

Elisabeth coloured under his gaze. "I know, I know," she said lightly, trying to pass it off as a jest, "you find me far too forward."

"No," he countered seriously. "I find you utterly delightful."

Suddenly it seemed as if everything were happening far too swiftly for Elisabeth. Indeed, they had already reached the park and it was, as Somerton had predicted, virtually deserted. He pulled up his horses and handed the reins over to his groom.

"Will you walk about the grounds with me, Miss Henrick?" he said very formally. When she hesitated, a smile appeared and he said softly, "Craven?"

Simpering, Elisabeth retaliated, "Oh, sir, how can you think such a thing? Merely because what you suggest outrages all sense of propriety? For without my chaperone and you a man of *such* reputation . . ."

Instantly Somerton matched her tone. "Oh, Miss Henrick, will it soothe your sensibilities, quell your qualms, if I give you my assurances—

word of a gentleman—that I shall offer you no insult, take no liberties with your person?"

Her eyes dancing with unspoken laughter, Elisabeth replied seriously, "Oh, sir, indeed you have set all my fears at rest."

Once upon the path, however, Elisabeth's mood turned genuinely serious. Darnell could not fail to note the change. "My parents did not overset you?" he asked with some concern. "My father, in particular, is wont to be quite daunting, at times. But no one could be kinder when there is a need. Or a better person to turn to if one is in difficulty," he added deliberately.

Elisabeth ignored the implication of the last few words and smiled. "I quite liked both of them," she told Darnell frankly.

He regarded the top of her head for several moments and then said, with a frown, "You were not distressed by the talk of your father's ... bastards?" She shook her head without looking at him, and he went on, "No one would think to hold you to account for his behaviour."

"You are ... very generous," Elisabeth replied, unable to keep a trace of bitterness out of her voice.

Darnell stopped and placed a hand on each of Elisabeth's shoulders. "I have spoken the truth," he said curtly. "You are a woman I respect and admire and desire, very much."

Startled, Elisabeth's eyes flew up to meet his. "Are ... are you offering me a *carte blanche?*" she stammered at last.

It was Somerton's turn to be stunned. "I neither know nor care what madness would lead you to ask such a thing. But I am offering you marriage," he said from between clenched teeth. "To me. When and where you choose. Will you marry me, Miss Henrick?"

Elisabeth looked up at him, wanting very much to throw her arms about his neck and say "Yes!" But as she looked at him, she knew she could not. She loved him far too much to chain him to a woman such as herself, for she could not believe that he would make such an offer if he knew the truth of her past. At last she pulled herself free and turned away. "I cannot," she said. It was almost a sob.

Behind her, hands on hips, Darnell demanded curtly, "Why not?"

"The . . . the ceremony. I cannot bear large weddings," she said wildly.

"I shall procure a *special license*. Tomorrow, if you wish. Then we may be married as quietly as you wish, where you wish," Darnell told her impatiently.

Elisabeth placed one hand against a tree to steady herself. Still she refused to look at Somerton. "I cannot," she repeated desperately.

"Why not?" he asked again. "I had not thought I was so lacking in address or deficient in understanding as to be unacceptable as a husband."

"Perhaps it is I who is deficient in understanding," she said, a quaver in her voice.

"Perhaps," he agreed amiably as he leaned against another tree. *That* made her laugh. Then, treacherously, he came forward and took her hands in his and said, "What is it, my love? You are not such a pea goose as to believe these things need stand in our way. What, then, is the matter?"

As he stared down at her so kindly, Elisabeth felt her eyes fill with tears. "I . . . I cannot explain it," she said.

Slowly, so that she might have time to object if she chose, Darnell took Elisabeth in his arms. "Am I so detestable to you?" he asked gently. "You need only tell me so." She shook her head. "Have I spoken too soon?" he persisted.

Gratefully, Elisabeth seized on that. "Yes. Give me time to know my own mind," she said. "I had not expected—"

She broke off and Darnell nodded. Then, slowly, he kissed her. To his delight, and her mortification, she did not pull away. And it was in that moment that he knew. Darnell could not have said how he knew, but unmistakably he knew. So intent was Elisabeth on the feel of his arms about her, she did not hear the soft intake of breath as he realised that the woman he held was—must be—Harriet Tremaine. So that is why she won't marry me, he told himself silently; why she so rarely speaks of her past.

For a moment Darnell was tempted to say what he thought aloud, but in the end he did not. It was not for lack of certainty but because he cherished the foolish hope that she would, one day, tell him herself. It did not occur to Somerton to ask himself why she had undertaken such a masquerade. In the weeks he had danced attendance upon Miss Henrick he had come to know her well enough to know that whatever the reason, it must have been a compelling one, and one that could only do her credit. So it was that he gently detached himself, several minutes later, and slowly walked her back to his carriage. "I shall remember what you said about large ceremonies and procure a special license. In the event you change your mind and say you *will* marry me," he hastened to add. "But we need not use it. I should be equally content to post the banns. I shall also write to your father. I ought to have done so before I spoke to you, of course, but I was, you see, devilish impatient."

Elisabeth turned to him and said urgently, "Oh, but there is no need to write my father! He is . . . I am of age."

"As you wish," he agreed courteously. In this, too, he was determined not to press her.

They had still not reached the carriage and Elisabeth coloured deeply as she said, "What just occurred . . . I have, I know, behaved with the greatest impropriety and must make you think me half-mad that I could respond so and yet not know my own mind about marriage."

She looked at him questioningly and he gave her a reassuring smile. "You needn't fear," he said seriously. "Whatever occurred, I could not think less than the best of you."

"You are very kind," Elisabeth said, not knowing quite how to answer him.

"Elisabeth," he began. He paused and then added, "I shall always have the highest regard for you, whatever you decide. But if ever you feel the need to confide in me, I shall be here, and please believe I should do whatever was in my power to serve you."

Elisabeth could not speak, and moments later Darnell handed her into the phaeton. With a courteous smile for his groom, Somerton took the reins. Then, without the least trace of distress at her refusal, Darnell amused Elisabeth with various *on-dits* until they reached the Henrick residence. There he saw her safely inside before returning to his own family's townhouse.

His father, of course, was waiting for him. In response to the unspoken question, Somerton said curtly, "I don't know. For the moment, at least, she has turned me down."

9

Elisabeth watched as Letty applied the elder-berry juice to her eyebrows and lashes. "Never," Letty said judiciously, "allow your artifices to be so obvious that men become aware of them. They much prefer to believe that the bloom in your cheek is natural—no matter how unlikely that may be!"

As her aunt applied the alkanna root salve to her lips, Elisabeth replied fretfully, "I can scarcely suppose it will matter, in my case."

Letty turned to stare directly at her niece. "My dear, it *always* matters." She paused and sighed. "Somerton, I suppose. Nothing else would make you look like that. Has he begun to tire of you?"

"Worse!" Elisabeth retorted tragically. "He has asked me to marry him."

Letitia regarded her niece with the liveliest astonishment. "And *that* has overset you? I know I said it most unlikely that he would, but I should have expected you to be delighted. Unless you suspect him of trifling with you. Casting out lures he does not intend to honour, perhaps?"

Elisabeth shook her head and took a deep breath. Unaccountably she found it difficult to meet Letty's eyes. "No, I think he quite meant what he said. He truly wishes to marry me. But what am I to tell him? Of my history, I mean. That he met me on a boat more than a year ago? That I was a governess then? That I am therefore outrageously eccentric? For so he must think unless I tell him what drove me to such a course. And what, then? What if I tell him the truth, that I did so because my father had made life at home intolerable for me? Will he wish to ally himself with such a line? Will he even hold me blameless? My mother did not."

"Tell him nothing," Letty advised with a shrug. "He may not think to ask."

Elisabeth began to pace about the room. "I cannot, Aunt Letty! I will not serve him such a backhanded turn. How I wish I had never begun the masquerade of Harriet Tremaine! But what other course of action was there? Not a one of my relatives could I have gone to, except Marietta and Hugh, but she was breeding."

Hearing the questions that had become so familiar to both of them, Letitia answered very bluntly. "There was no other course for you to take. We did, most discreetly, of course, write some of your other relatives, you know. None of them wanted the responsibility."

"I know," Elisabeth agreed with a sigh. "But why couldn't my mother have helped me, before she died, instead of leaving me the money afterwards?"

Letty bit her lower lip. "You know what she was: all gentle helplessness. She did her best: sent you off to school and then, once you were too old for that, sent you off on a round of visits to family. It was only when she grew so sick herself that she brought you home. And by then, well, I do not think her mind was always of the clearest, nor her understanding ever more than moderate. Be grateful she made provision for you in her will. And that her father, before her, tied up the money away from your father so that it was there for your mother to bequeath you."

"I am grateful," Elisabeth said quietly. "And I suppose I should even be grateful that my parents were so careful to keep my disappearance a secret. But I cannot help thinking it was for the sake of their own reputations that they did so."

Calmly Letitia applied Spanish wool to her cheeks with the softest of brushes. "At least they did so. But you cannot change the past, so let us consider the future. How do you intend to answer Somerton?"

It was Elisabeth's turn to shrug. "I don't know. I can neither tell him the truth nor marry him without doing so. I love him too much for that."

Letty sighed. "I do wish, occasionally, that you had not inherited so many scruples! It is no part of my plans to see you dwindle into an old maid, my dear."

Elisabeth smiled affectionately at her aunt. "Don't worry, I shall come about yet, I promise you."

"Good!" Letty said, rising from her dressing-table. "Now, Elisabeth, I am expecting a gentleman, so you must be off. And do try, my dear, not to come again unless you absolutely must. I am always happy to see you, of course, but I fear the risk you run. Should anyone guess, you would be ruined."

Elisabeth nodded and pulled the boy's cap lower over her head. "I understand," she said with a sigh.

"Good," Letty repeated, patting her niece's cheek. "And now I must find some oil and warm it up. Marcus adores being rubbed all over with warm oil."

Elisabeth chuckled as she left. It was, no doubt, precisely this sort of thing that made Letitia so popular with the gentlemen. Indeed, there were those who said Letty outshone even the legendary Harriet Wilson. Who was, Elisabeth reminded herself sternly, someone she was not even supposed to know about!

Unfortunately, Elisabeth's good mood could not persist. Marietta, who was to have gone to a concert that evening, had returned early and she discovered Elisabeth slipping in through the back door. "Good God, child, where have you been?" Marietta demanded as she hustled Elisabeth up to her room. "If any of the servants see you, we are done for!"

With a bravura she was far from feeling, Elisabeth retorted, "Would you rather I visited Aunt Letty dressed as myself?"

The door to Elisabeth's room safely shut behind her, Marietta could only sink into a chair and whisper, "Aunt Letty? Aunt Letty? You've been to see Letitia Roxbury?"

Without haste, Elisabeth set about changing from her groom's outfit to a dressing gown. "I have already said so."

"But why?"

Elisabeth paused to look directly at her cousin. "Aunt Letty has been a part of my life ever since I can remember. And though I know the *ton* must disapprove, I cannot and will not give her the cut. As I have no wish, however, to be recognised and have my credit utterly destroyed, I go dressed as a boy."

"But ... but does Letitia actually encourage you in this madness?" Marietta demanded. "I cannot believe it of her! However careless she is of her own reputation, surely she is not heedless of yours?"

Elisabeth looked away. Impossible to explain. Impossible even to tell Marietta the reason she had need of Letty's advice. Harriet Tremaine must remain a secret. Elisabeth could only shrug lightly and say, "No, she is as troubled as you that I take such risks."

"Then have done with them!" Marietta retorted firmly. "If what you have said is true, then Letitia will understand perfectly." She paused, and her voice was stern when she spoke again. "You are in my care, Elisabeth. I must ask you to promise me that you will not see your Aunt Letty again."

Calmly Elisabeth replied, "I promise, cousin, that I shall not see her again unless I absolutely must."

Seeing the set of Elisabeth's chin, Marietta was forced to be content. She knew Elisabeth far too well to believe the girl could be forced to alter her position. And, after all, Marietta consoled herself, just what could there be that would require Elisabeth to visit Letitia?

Elisabeth watched as Marietta's face reflected her thoughts. "Please don't worry," she said impulsively. "Indeed, I promise I shall give you no further cause for alarm."

Marietta smiled wanly and wagged a finger at her cousin. "Well, I shall hold you to that promise!" She paused and then said, rather diffidently, "You know, my dear, Mr. Somerton has grown very particular in his attentions towards you, of late. Several ladies of my acquaintance have remarked upon it. With any other gentleman I would expect an offer to be forthcoming, but with Mr. Somerton . . . Well, I confess I wonder if I ought to hint him away? Or . . . or at least ask his intentions."

"No!" As Marietta looked at her in surprise, Elisabeth blushed and said, "I . . . he . . . that is, there is no need."

Marietta stared at her cousin. After a moment she shrugged. "Perhaps you are right. He may yet come up to scratch. Very well, we shall give him time. Gentlemen always stick at actually making an offer, but we may bring him round. Though I cannot think it likely," she added sternly. "Now to bed with you! Recollect that some of your old school friends are coming to call on you in the morning."

"To be sure. Good night, Marietta. Sleep well."

"I know I shall lie awake for hours," Marietta countered with conviction. Retreating to the door, she added, "No one could be having a worse evening than I!"

In this Marietta was mistaken. At that precise moment, Mr. Darnell Somerton stood beside the fireplace in the drawing-room of the Duke of Carston's London townhouse. He was dressed in evening attire, as was his companion, the Duchess of Carston. She had dressed, in fact, with great forethought, in silvery lace and satin, and her hair and face were dressed with as much care as ever Letitia Roxbury might employ. And yet the sight appeared to afford Mr. Somerton no pleasure. "Why have you asked me here, Pamela?" he demanded curtly.

The duchess disposed herself on a sofa before she answered, careful to allow a generous portion of ankle to show beneath the hem of her dress. With a graceful turn of her wrist, Pamela indicated the green-and-gold drawing-room around her. "Beautiful, isn't it?" she asked softly. "One would have thought it would be impossible to be unhappy here. But I am, Darry." She paused and Somerton merely regarded her politely. The duchess rose to her feet and paced about the room. "You cannot conceive of my loneliness," she told him, a quaver in her voice.

"I fail to see how this concerns me," Darnell replied coolly. "Or why you asked me to come here tonight."

With superb grace the duchess turned, and without having intended it, Darnell found her in his arms. She looked up at him, eyes liquid with unshed tears. "Because I feel so helpless," she whispered. "Because I've come to see that my marriage was a dreadful mistake and that I ought to have married you, Darry! Oh, Darry, if you were to ask me to come away with you, now, anywhere, I would do it!"

Carefully, Somerton set her aside. Then, very quietly, he replied, "But I am not asking you, Pamela."

"Why not?" she demanded tearfully.

He half-turned away. "Because you *are* married, however disagreeable you find that state to be. You were neither tricked nor forced into *this* marriage, Pamela. It was one of your own choosing."

With a catch in her voice, the duchess demanded, "Are you never going to forgive me for that, Darry?"

Somerton placed his hands on her shoulders. "It is not a matter of forgiving," he said quietly. "It is simply a fact that you *are* married."

"I could divorce him," Pamela suggested coolly, her eyes searching Darnell's.

He shook his head. "Do so, if you must, but not for me. The time when we might have made a match of it is past."

Angrily the duchess pulled free and paced once more. "It's that Henrick girl, isn't it?" she demanded bluntly. "You've a *tendre* for her, haven't you? Do you know they are laying bets at White's that you are to be leg-shackled at last? Well, I shall laugh to see it! You! No doubt she will be grateful to you for taking her off the shelf, and indeed, it is not as if she had any other hope of wedding wealth or title. I wish you joy of your spinster!"

Somerton regarded her for a long moment before he spoke. "Give over this bitterness, Pamela. However much you may profess to detest your new title and wealth, you must know they are as important to you as ever. What is forty thousand pounds a year compared to eighty thousand? And viscount to duke? If you ran away with me, you would regret it before three months were out. Stay with your duke. He is even, I understand, willing to tolerate your little affairs, so long as you are discreet. And, as I recall, you *can* be very discreet."

The Duchess of Carston could not at once answer, she was so enraged. Finally she hissed, "Get out of here! I hate you!"

And with that she threw her slipper to speed him on his way. It had not been, Darnell felt as he made good his escape, a very enjoyable evening. Behind him, the duchess was in the process of expressing aloud the same sentiments, only in far stronger terms!

—10—

Elisabeth woke with a start. The nightmares had been coming with greater frequency of late, and it was several moments before she could cease shaking. As her breath began to come more normally, there was a rap at the door and the maid entered carrying a cup of chocolate and a few biscuits. Setting the small tray on the table beside Elisabeth's bed, the girl began to chatter. "It's a beautiful day, it is, Miss Elisabeth. All sun and wind. They do say we've been having an uncommonly good spring. Oh, and Mr. Henrick said to tell you he'll be in the breakfast-room another half-hour, no more, and he'd like to see you. Business to attend to, I don't doubt."

At this news, Elisabeth hastily rose, dressed, and practically flew downstairs, directing the maid to take the chocolate and biscuits away. Hugh Henrick looked up with pleasure as his cousin entered the breakfast-room. He was, of course, alone, for Marietta preferred to lie abed.

"Did you wish to see me?" Elisabeth asked a trifle breathlessly.

Hugh Henrick set aside the paper he had been reading and eyed his young cousin sharply. "Marietta tells me you have been visiting Letitia," he said sternly. She nodded and he went on, with a sigh, "Well, I cannot find it in me to fault you for it. I see Letitia, from time to time, myself. But you *do* understand that it won't do for you to, don't you? At any rate not until you're safely wed. All the tattle-boxes in London would take up the tale if they knew of it."

Elisabeth smiled and patted her cousin's hand. "I understand, Hugh, and give you my word I shall not do so lightly."

Hugh cleared his throat. "Well, that's all right, then. Tell me, Elisabeth, are you happy here? Enjoying yourself?"

"Very much, sir," Elisabeth told him warmly. "And I am very grateful to you and Marietta for bringing me out."

"Nonsense!" Hugh said stoutly. "Happy to do it. And the children adore having you to play with. Point of fact, I believe you're spoiling them. What's this about taking them to Astley's Amphitheatre?"

Elisabeth laughed. "Well, they did so very much want to go, and I could not bring myself to deny them the treat." She paused and smiled mischievously at her cousin. "To tell the truth, I own I enjoyed myself as much as any of the children."

"Well, I can't say I'm sorry you took them," Hugh conceded amiably. "But you are to remember that you came to visit us for your own pleasure and not to be plagued to death by my offspring!"

"No fear of that, I assure you," Elisabeth said with another laugh.

"Good. Well, I must be off, my dear," he said, rising from the table. "And remember, if

you need anything and your purse won't stand
the nonsense, you are to charge it to me."

Elisabeth nodded and watched him go, feeling a strong affection for her cousin. It was
this, combined with the knowledge that her
friends were coming, that gave Elisabeth a sense
of security. She was no closer to knowing what
to say to Darnell Somerton when next they
met, but for the moment she could believe that
there was an answer.

Several hours later, Elisabeth stood in her
room. Her friends had come and gone, leaving
her with a warm glow. She was, Elisabeth knew,
alone in the house, save for the servants, for
Marietta had gone out directly after lunch,
and it was a peaceful notion. Nor did she feel
any qualms when the maid rapped on her door
to tell her, "Miss Elisabeth, there's a gentleman below wishing to speak with you or Mrs.
Henrick."

"I shall be there directly," Elisabeth replied.
"Show him into the drawing-room."

For a moment her heart raced as she wondered if Darnell had come to call. But she
dismissed that pleasant notion in a trice, for,
had it been he, the maid would have said so.
Mr. Somerton was, after all, a frequent caller
these days. Curious, but scarcely alarmed, Elisabeth entered the drawing-room only to hastily shut the doors behind her as she realised
who was there. "Father!"

John Henrick slowly turned and faced the
daughter he had not seen in more than six
years. He was as tall as she remembered him,
and as handsome. There was a ruggedness about
his face that suggested he knew very well what
he wanted and how to get it. Not even the

carelessness of his clothes could detract from the impact he made. He let out a long, slow breath. "Elisabeth," he said quietly, "it's been a long time."

"Yes, it has," she agreed evenly.

"Your mother died asking for you. You broke her heart, you know." The words were spoken as if with gentle sorrow.

Elisabeth looked at her father, feeling the old guilt once more begin to overwhelm her. Nevertheless, she forced herself to say, curtly, "I am sorry she suffered, Father, but you know very well why I could not be there."

John Henrick came forward and took his daughter's hands in his. "No, Elisabeth, I don't know," he said gently. "I only know you fancied something wrong and ran away. But that's all over now. I've come to take you home, to take care of you. If you're still afraid or upset, well, we'll call in doctors. The best we can find to deal with your nervousness."

"No!" she said, pulling free. In panic she fled to a far corner of the room, where she turned and faced her father. "No! I won't go with you. I'll stay here with Hugh and Marietta. Perhaps I'll even marry. But whatever happens, I won't go home with you!"

Henrick shook his head sadly. "Oh, Elisabeth! How can you imagine I would allow any man to take your hand in marriage? Knowing what I do about the strange fancies you have? Suppose you had children and passed on this madness to them?"

"Get out!" Elisabeth flung the words at him. "Just get out of my life."

"I can't. You are, after all, my daughter," he said, advancing on her.

As he came closer, Elisabeth drew herself up to her full height. With a quiet dignity she said, "I am of age. You cannot force me to come home with you and I will not go."

"No?" The word was sinister in his use of it. "The alternative is Bedlam, you know. If not now, then in a few years. Indeed, I am going there, today, to speak to them about your case. But I would much prefer to keep you at home with me. Think about it, Elisabeth. I shall return in a few days and I shall expect you to be ready to go with me then."

He gave her a long, steady look and then turned to leave. Without moving, Elisabeth watched him. Only when she heard the outer door open and shut again did she allow herself to sink into a chair, not even aware she was crying. Impossible to believe he was actually gone! Six years and she felt scarcely more able to deal with him now than she had then. He meant his threat, of that she was sure. The only thing incomprehensible to Elisabeth was that her father had given her a reprieve, a few days before he would return.

A few days. As those words penetrated Elisabeth's mind, she was moved to action and fairly flew upstairs. Frantically she searched for the clothes she wore to visit Letty. But they were not where she kept them and Elisabeth realised that Marietta must have taken them. Pacing about her room, ELisabeth tried to think. Ought she to send a note to Letty? To what purpose? She stopped pacing and looked out the window. To what purpose, indeed? To begin another masquerade? To spend more years of her life running and hiding? To forfeit everything she had gained in the past year?

Slowly Elisabeth realised that she could not do it. No more than she could tamely go home with her father. But if not, then there was only one other alternative open to her. Almost as if she were in a dream, Elisabeth sat down at her writing desk and composed a note to Mr. Darnell Somerton. Within half an hour it was safely dispatched and Elisabeth waited nervously for the reply. Whatever the impropriety of her behaviour, she was determined to see it through.

Elisabeth did not have long to wait. Darnell chose to reply in person, and scarcely an hour after her father had left, Somerton was admitted to see Miss Henrick. Rising to meet him, Elisabeth held out a hand. "Thank you for coming, sir," she said warmly.

Darnell took the hand in both of his, searching her face. "What is it, Miss Henrick?" he asked with concern. "What has happened to overset you?"

Ignoring his question, Elisabeth stammered, "I know I ought not to say this, but do you still wish to marry me?"

Somerton's frown of concern turned to something else, something far warmer. "Need you ask?" he demanded huskily.

Her eyes met his and held them for several long moments. "Do you mean that?" The question was for herself as much as for him. "If you do, then my answer is yes."

Letting go of Elisabeth's hand, Darnell drew her into his arms and brought his lips down on hers, hungrily. To his utter delight, she responded eagerly. After a moment he let her go and said, still huskily, "When?"

Elisabeth stammered again. "As—as soon as

you like. By special license, perhaps? You . . . you did say you meant to procure one."

Puzzled, Darnell looked down at his bride-to-be. "I have it here, in my pocket," he said slowly. "If you truly wish it, we could be married today."

"Today?" Startled, Elisabeth twisted her hands together. "But there is Marietta. I must tell her first. And Hugh. I should like them to be present."

Somerton took Elisabeth's chin in one hand and turned her face to look up at him. "We shall be married when and where you will," he said. "If you crave a church wedding with family and a few friends, that still need take only a few days. We shall give out, if you wish, that my devilish impatience is the cause for our unseemly haste."

"Could we?" she asked him anxiously. "You will not regret it later if we do?"

In answer, Darnell kissed her again. It was an extremely astonished Marietta who entered the drawing-room a few minutes later and discovered the couple still embracing. *"Elisabeth! Mr. Somerton!"* she cried in outrage. "Stop that this instant!" As the couple complied, Marietta fanned herself with one hand. "Have you no sense of decency?" she demanded. "Go upstairs, Elisabeth, I shall speak to you later. You have utterly sunk yourself beyond reproach with your behaviour. And you, Mr. Somerton, I—"

Neatly Somerton cut her short. "And *I,* Mrs. Henrick, am engaged to your cousin."

"Engaged?" Marietta looked at Elisabeth with the liveliest astonishment.

Elisabeth nodded and Darnell took her hand

to steady her. "We shall be married in a day or two," he said smoothly. "I already have a special license and we would both prefer a small wedding."

"But—but your father, Elisabeth," Marietta protested finally. "When did he give his consent?"

For a moment, a look of bleakness crossed Elisabeth's face. Then she said quietly, "You forget I am of age, Marietta. He . . . he would not wish to come, anyway."

Faintly Marietta managed a smile. "Well, I am very happy for you, my dear," she said a trifle tremulously. "And no one could say it was a mean match, could they? That is, if you are quite sure, Mr. Somerton?"

"I am," he told her kindly. "And I wish everyone would cease to find that so surprising."

"But such haste," Marietta persisted.

Darnell bowed and in his haughtiest tone replied, "The blame lies with me, Mrs. Henrick. I find that I do not choose to wait."

"Well," Marietta said helplessly, "I see nothing for it but to wish you happy!"

Viscount and Lady Langston took the news of Darnell's engagement far more calmly. They had, after all, had some warning of the matter. Nevertheless, even they were unprepared for the announcement that the wedding would take place within three days. "Two, if I can arrange for the use of a church that quickly," Darnell amended blandly.

Viscount Langston studied his son's face, then turned to his wife and said, "He don't look as if he's queer in his attic. Very well, Darry, we shall back you on this if you wish it."

"Thank you, sir."

There seemed nothing more to say and Darnell took his leave. When he was gone, Lady Langston turned to her husband and said thoughtfully, "You don't suppose the poor girl is in trouble, do you?"

"If she is," the viscount answered firmly, "I'll lay odds it ain't her fault. She's pluck to the backbone, that one, and honest as well. Breeding always tells."

—11—

Marriage. Numbly Elisabeth whispered that word to herself and looked around the room, trying to shake off the sense of unreality that had gripped her for two days now. A rap at the door helped. It was Marietta come to help her dress. "Oh, my dear, this is beyond everything I hoped for, for you," Marietta began with a sigh. "I only wish your father could be here."

And I am grateful he is not, Elisabeth told herself silently. Wherever he was, she hoped he would not appear until the knot was safely tied and she and Darnell were out of London! Though even then, the problem would not be resolved, only postponed.

Something of this must have shown on Elisabeth's face, for Marietta asked a trifle anxiously, "You are not ill, I trust?" When Elisabeth shook her head, Marietta relaxed and added complacently, "Nerves, I've no doubt. Quite unexceptional, I assure you! Every bride is expected to suffer from them. On with your dress and you will feel better. I vow Suzette has outdone herself! Now where *are* those gloves?"

The offending articles were soon found, Elisabeth properly attired, and her hair dressed in the most elegant style Marietta's maid could

attain. Elisabeth was obliged to concede that
she was indeed beautiful.

But there was no time for wool-gathering.
Hugh must be called upon to admire Elisabeth's
dress and then the carriage was waiting outside.
Scarcely any time later, it seemed, she was
facing Darnell at the church, and he was looking gravely at her. Years later, Elisabeth would
find herself saying that she barely remembered
the ceremony or the breakfast at Hugh's townhouse afterwards. But at the moment, all she
could think of was Darnell's face. He must,
she knew, share some of the trepidation she
felt, but his face revealed nothing of the sort.
He looked at her with the politeness of a
stranger, but there was not the least hesitation
in his replies or in the way he placed the ring
upon her finger. And when he kissed her, it
was as though they both caught fire so that
their breath came in ragged gasps when he let
her go. Then it was time to leave the church
and a blur of congratulations followed. Only
Viscount Langston and his wife stood out in
her mind, marked by her surprise at the genuine affection with which they welcomed her to
the family. Would they be so kind, she could not
help wondering even then, amid the celebration,
if they knew the truth about her? But they did
not, and in any event, there was too much to do
to ponder such matters just then.

Soon, too soon, perhaps, Elisabeth found herself dressed in travelling clothes and in a carriage with Darnell. "Hello, Mrs. Somerton,"
he said with a quiet smile when they had pulled
away from the curb and all their well-wishers.

And with that Darnell was once again the
man she had grown so fond of, and Elisabeth

found she was no longer afraid of him. She held out her hand and smiled. Indeed, her eyes danced a little as she said, demurely, "It's a long journey we've begun, Mr. Somerton."

He smiled as well, but his voice was grave as he replied, "Between us we shall make it a very pleasant one, I hope."

"Do you know," Elisabeth said warmly, "most men, I should think, would have said they would do *their* best to make it a pleasant one! How grateful I am that you said 'we,' for I do look upon it as a joint venture."

"If I thought you did not, I should scarcely have married you," Darnell shot back with a grin.

Without a word, Elisabeth switched seats so that, instead of facing him, she was beside Darnell. She tucked her small, gloved hand into the crook of his elbow and said, somewhat ruefully, "Do you know, I haven't the slightest notion where we are going? Save that it appears to be out of London."

Darnell smiled. "True. In the rush of the past few days there has been no time to consult you. We are going to Paris. Have you ever been there, my love?" Elisabeth shook her head and he went on, "I was, before Napoleon slipped his leash, and I am looking forward to showing it to you. And showing *you* to Paris."

"I shall like it above all things," Elisabeth replied happily.

"Shall you?" Darnell said with a grin. "How splendid for you."

Elisabeth laughed at the reminder of that drive that now seemed so long ago. "And how fortunate, no doubt," she added dryly, "for I collect you've already made all the arrangements?"

"I have," he confirmed. "But I should change them in a moment if they displeased you," he told her gallantly.

"A fine thing that would be," Elisabeth retorted cheerfully, "if I were to set you under the cat's paw this early in our marriage!"

"I doubt if you could!" he shot back at once.

"Is that a challenge?"

"Scarcely," he answered dryly. "I've told you at least once before that I've no desire to cross swords with you. A partnership is more what I have a mind for." He paused and looked out the window. "We shall reach the coast by nightfall," he said, "and sail in the morning, if the day is clear."

"And if it is not?" she asked.

A gleam appeared in his eyes as Darnell answered, "Why, Mrs. Somerton, I'll wager we shall find a way to pass the time." Elisabeth blushed and he added, "Indeed, if I did not know you were such an excellent sailor, I might hope for a day that, while not intolerable, would still cause us to dally a day on shore."

At his last words, Elisabeth went pale and her voice was scarcely above a whisper as she said, "What do you mean? How can you know whether I am an excellent sailor or not?"

Almost Somerton told her the truth, that he had guessed who she must have been before her come-out. But the sight of her frightened face looking up at him stayed him. Not for the world would he distress her further if she could not yet bring herself to tell him the truth. Still, he tried to calm her fears. "Forgive me, Elisabeth. I had forgotten I have never seen you sail. It must be that you remind me of someone I once met."

"It . . . it seems a common occurrence, these days," she said hesitatingly. "Everyone seems to think they have met me, somewhere."

Darnell did not at once reply. "I am sorry if I have distressed you," he said at last.

Elisabeth looked away, hating the need to lie, and yet unable to risk everything now. "My father's legacy is everywhere, it seems," she said softly, more to herself than to her husband.

But Darnell heard her. Just as quietly he said, "You cannot be held to account for your father's excesses. And while he is still not well-liked, it may help to know that your father has been accounted quite faithful to your mother. My father tells me there was never the least whisper that he had ever looked at another lady after he married her."

Elisabeth continued to look away. Silently the bitterness flowed over her. Not the least breath of scandal? How could there be when her parents worshipped their reputations? Her father was discreet, one had always to allow him that. Young country servants and family, that had been where he cast his eyes. Girls, scarcely women yet, who would not dare to report what had occurred.

But of course Elisabeth could not speak her thoughts aloud. Something compelled her to ask, however, "What was she like? The girl I resemble?"

"I scarcely know," Darnell replied coolly. "My acquaintance with her was of the slightest. I can only tell you that she was quite out of the common way."

"A member of the *demi-monde,* perhaps?" Elisabeth suggested, curious to hear his reply.

"No, she was a governess. Or so she said, and I had no reason to doubt her."

Her eyes carefully fixed on her hands, Elisabeth asked quietly, "A governess? How odd! How did she come your way?"

"By accident," he said quietly. "Shall I also allow that I kissed her?"

Elisabeth's eyes flew up to meet his. "That . . . that seems an odd thing to tell me," she said, but her voice held no anger.

Darnell took her hands in his. "I know it is, my dear, but I begin as I mean to go on—in honesty. I kissed her because she seemed utterly desirable to me. But not so desirable as you are, my wife, my love."

Before she could realise what he was about, Darnell had swept Elisabeth up into a passionate embrace. Elisabeth felt a sense of tremendous joy in being able, at last, to do what she had wanted to do from the first time she saw his face. And without the least impropriety!

As Elisabeth clung to Darnell, her mouth eagerly meeting his, his hands explored the buttons of her pelisse and slipped inside to caress her breasts. Elisabeth moaned with the warmth of sensations she had never known before, and his hands moved lower to explore the outlines of her body through the fabric of her dress. Her own hands gripped his shoulders, delighting in their strength and, almost, Elisabeth feared she would faint as Darnell stroked the triangle between her thighs.

With a ragged laugh, Darnell abruptly pulled away. "I am forgetting where we are, my love. I think we'd best wait."

Elisabeth placed her hands over his. "Where and when you will," she said.

Where turned out to be a prosperous posting-house on the road to the coast, for they did not make as good time as Darnell had hoped. *When* was after a very private supper.

"I shall see that everything is arranged for tomorrow," Darnell told his bride with smouldering eyes. "Go on to bed."

Elisabeth nodded. "Very well. I shall be waiting."

When Darnell followed her, scarcely thirty minutes later, he found her seated before a fire that burned in the room's small hearth. Her hair was down and it caught the fire's light as she brushed it. She wore, moreover, a shift of the sheerest, finest lawn Darnell had ever seen, and she seemed not in the least abashed at everything it revealed. Without words he crossed the room and Elisabeth rose to meet him. Once more his arms held her: searching, stroking, kindling a fire in both of them as his mouth closed over hers.

Suddenly, Darnell swung Elisabeth off her feet and carried her to the four-poster bed whose covers had already been turned back. As though he could not bear to let her go, one of Darnell's hands continued to hold Elisabeth as the other tore at his cravat.

"Allow me," Elisabeth murmured mischievously, and her hands reached for his waistcoat.

Darnell did not demur and soon that and his cravat and coat and shirt were all discarded in a crumpled heap upon the floor. A few moments later his breeches lay on the floor with the rest of his clothes. Hungrily, Darnell stroked Elisabeth's nipples through the thin material

of her shift and she moaned in anticipation.
Then his hands were reaching for, gently
exploring, the wet, lovely space between her
thighs. Scarcely knowing what she was about,
Elisabeth reached for his manhood softly pleading, "Please!"

A movement here, a shift in weight there,
and Darnell was on top of her, gently spread-
ing Elisabeth's thighs apart. The pain as he
thrust inside, spurred now by his own needs,
was over in a moment. As he thrust deeper
and deeper, Elisabeth felt as though she would
be split in two by the exquisite pleasure and,
together, they crested.

Cradled safely in his arms, a little later,
Elisabeth seemed scarcely real to Darnell, and
he reached out to stroke her long hair spread
all over his chest. Elisabeth only snuggled
deeper in the curve of his arm. The fire caught
his eye, and with a curious smile he asked
Elisabeth why she had kindled it.

Her forefinger traced a path through the
hair on Darnell's chest. "For the warmth,"
she said demurely. "My shift was so fine and
I had not known how much heat we would
create between ourselves." With her last words,
Elisabeth raised her eyes to meet Darnell's
and he could clearly read the challenge in
them.

"Jade!" he told her without rancour.

"Do you know, I think I should quite like to
dally here, tomorrow, fair weather or foul,"
she added softly.

With a laugh, Darnell swept her up atop
him and once more they became oblivious to
everything save themselves and each other.

Sometime later, when Darnell had already fallen asleep, Elisabeth could not help thinking that this had been the most wonderful day she had ever known.

—12—

Summer. 1816. Mr. and Mrs. Somerton returned to a London that was virtually deserted. Which suited the pair, who found that quiet visits with friends were preferable to the incessant activity of the Season just past. Some of Darnell's bachelor friends came prepared to dislike the new Mrs. Somerton. One of these was Sir Peter Dunsworth. Encountering Somerton at White's one day, he was startled into saying, "Darry! Devilish good to see you here! Wasn't expecting it, you know."

"Peter! Where the devil have *you* been? Didn't see you at all, this past Season. Someone told me you were rusticating—seemed deuced unlike you."

Sir Peter made a face. "S'truth. M'sister had it in her head to matchmake and I'd no notion to be wasting m'time doing the pretty to a bunch of wretched chits! So I went off to visit some friends up north. Had quite a merry time of it, Darry. You'd be amazed what they can get up to when they choose. Far more fun than a Season, I tell you! But, hey, what's this I hear? You leg-shackled? Tenant-for-life? With the Henrick girl?"

Darnell grinned. "Yes, it's true. Come and meet her. Today, if you like."

Something of Dunsworth's good humour seemed to dim. "Well, uh, I . . . that is—"

Darnell raised an eyebrow. "Come, come, Peter, what is it? And no roundaboutation, either!"

Dunsworth scarcely hesitated before he spluttered, "Oh, very well! Dashed shame, I think it, to see *you* shackled. Never expected it. All these years, females setting their caps at you and none of 'em getting more than a glance. And the one Season I'm not around, you up and get married! Under the cat's paw, by now, I expect. Everyone says she set her cap at you shamelessly. Dash it, Darry, I don't know whether to congratulate you or to hold a wake! She ain't breeding, is she?"

Somerton knew Dunsworth too well to take offence and replied mildly, "So far as I know, she is not. I repeat: come and meet Elisabeth. Once you do, I think you'll understand. Might even give you a taste for the married state."

Alarmed, Dunsworth backed away. "No! There, I say. Doing it much too brown, Darry! Haven't any wish to be leg-shackled and can't imagine wanting to be."

Darnell grinned. "You needn't be so afraid. Come and meet her as a favour to me, then."

"Well . . ." Dunsworth hesitated. "I'm pledged to Charles for cards tonight."

"Come for tea," Darnell suggested.

"*Tea?*" Dunsworth blanched. "Muddle my insides with tea? Are you daft?"

"Just come," Darnell said, allowing a trace of laughter to creep into his voice. "I shall warrant for it that you need not drink tea. Or are you craven?"

Sir Peter straightened and threw back his shoulders. "I shall be there at four," he said solemnly.

At precisely 4:05, Elisabeth Somerton entered the salon given over to Darry and herself for entertaining their friends. Lord and Lady Langston firmly believed that families successfully shared houses only when each had adequate privacy. And she and Darry had made it a custom to take tea there together, unless expressly summoned to take tea with Darnell's parents. The dress she wore was of jonquil silk and had been bought in Paris. Indeed, it was Darnell's favourite and he was hard put not to take her in his arms when she entered the room. Elisabeth took a step towards him, then realised that there was another gentleman present as well. "How do you do, sir?" she said, managing a friendly smile.

Dunsworth bowed frostily as Darnell said, "This is an old friend of mine, Sir Peter Dunsworth."

Without the least hesitation, Elisabeth held out her hand and said warmly, "I am delighted to meet you. My husband has spoken of you with affection." She paused and looked at him carefully, then bit back a laugh. "You will not be wanting anything so mawkish as tea, I suspect," she hazarded shrewdly. "Darry brought back quite a tolerable claret from France, if you would prefer that?"

Dunsworth's eyes began to sparkle. "Indeed I would. That is, if you wouldn't mind, Mrs. Somerton?"

This time Elisabeth did not try to hold back

her laughter. "I should be pleased," she told him frankly as she rang for a maid.

As Sir Peter relaxed, so too did Somerton. It could not be said that he regretted his marriage. Nevertheless, it was impossible for him to be unaware that the haste of his marriage was something of an *on-dit*. It pleased him, therefore, to see even such a confirmed misogamist as Peter melt before Elisabeth's charming manner.

Darnell leaned back in his chair and watched his wife, feeling a great deal of pride in the grace with which she moved. It reminded him, he thought with a grin, of the way she moved in bed. He had fallen in love with Elisabeth the way she was, but it seemed to Darnell that she had grown even more beautiful, more desirable since their marriage. He still sometimes caught a glimpse of something hidden in her gaze, but the look of fear that had occasionally haunted her before was gone. For a man who had become accustomed to the notion that his marriage, whenever it might occur, must mean a polite arrangement of convenience, such happiness as this seemed not quite real. Darnell had ceased to question what it was about Elisabeth that made her so dear to him, he simply accepted that she was.

Elisabeth, looking over at her husband, caught a glimpse of what he was feeling. She smiled and neatly drew him into the conversation, then leaned back as Darnell and Sir Peter became engaged in a heated discussion of a certain aspirant of Gentleman Jackson's establishment. Due to her background as Miss Harriet Tremaine, she could follow tolerably well such points as "excellent bottom," "good science," "strips to advantage," and "a punishing left."

It was therefore with perfect truth that she could assure Sir Peter, when he paused anxiously to ask, that she was not in the least bored.

It was this virtue, perhaps, more than any other, that led Sir Peter to inform Darnell, "What a regular trojan she is! Mind you, marrying her may have been a bit extreme, but there it is! You always were impulsive, Darry. Still, if one must marry—"

"For the sake of heirs," Darnell interjected gravely.

"For the sake of heirs," Sir Peter agreed, equally gravely, "why, then, one could do far worse. Far worse, indeed."

The Duchess of Carston was privileged to hear these sentiments repeated in her presence a few days later. It was not that Sir Peter wished to cause trouble, you understand; it was simply that he could not abide the duchess. And when she tried to enlist his aid in arranging a rendez-vous with Darnell, Sir Peter quite frankly lost his temper and felt obliged to inform the duchess that he would scarcely lend himself to disrupting such a splendid union.

Pamela was not accustomed to such blunt speech, and the worst part was that she dared not treat Sir Peter as she would have liked. This was, perhaps, the moment in which her desire for revenge altered from something nebulous to something certain. It was the moment in which she realised the means to her end as well.

Mr. John Henrick, country gentleman that he had been most of his married life, was now to be seen in London again. Elisabeth Somerton was his daughter, but one had yet to hear that there was anything approaching cordiality between the pair. Indeed, Pamela knew quite well that John Henrick had not attended his daughter's wedding. Even now one might suppose she did not know he was in town.

It was therefore less than two hours later that Mr. Henrick received a discreet *billet* requesting him to call on her Grace, the Duchess of Carston, at his earliest convenience. To be frank, his first response was a shrug of contempt. He was not—no one could be—unaware of the lady's identity, and he considered her far too old for his tastes, however attractive other gentlemen might find her. Nor was he particularly impressed by nobility. Indeed, Mr. Henrick came very close to discarding the missive altogether. He did, however, possess a keen mind and he had scarcely relegated the poor lady to oblivion when he recalled that she was supposed to have an intimate interest in Darnell Somerton. At which point he became intrigued, for he was no more reconciled to his daughter's marriage than was Pamela.

Half an hour later, Mr. John Henrick was ushered into the Duchess of Carston's private drawing-room. The duke was nowhere to be seen. Pamela looked over her visitor with care and found little to cavil at in his coat of superfine and tan breeches. His boots bore a tolerable shine and his cravat revealed a creative, if a trifle careless hand. The face, moreover, was handsome, though lined with what might have been the evidence of dissipation. Green eyes met hers frankly and there seemed a touch of defiance in the careful dishevelment of his locks.

Without taking his eyes off the duchess, Henrick executed a flawless bow. "Your Grace," he murmured.

Pamela held out a hand and drew Henrick to a place on the sofa beside her. It amused the duchess to realise that Henrick's scrutiny of her was as exacting as her own had been. She was not distressed. Dressed in blue muslin with as much bosom bared as was seemly, a dainty foot peeping out from below her skirts, and hair dressed *à l'adrienne*, she was breathtakingly beautiful.

"Thank you for coming to see me," she said softly. "I hesitated to thrust myself so far forward, but . . . well, the matter is a delicate one—your daughter's marriage."

As Pamela watched, John Henrick's face tightened and rather curtly he said, "Indeed?"

The duchess looked down at her hands and continued in the same soft voice, "You will think it improper of me to say so, I know, but I cannot think the match an altogether . . . felicitous one."

Henrick's eyes narrowed as he replied, "I do not think it improper, but confess myself at a loss as to why you should think such a thing."

"Does the notion displease you?" Pamela asked, staking her plans on frankness.

For a moment Henrick did not answer. Instead, he studied the woman facing him. Curtly he said, at last, "Shall I be frank, your Grace? I am well aware that you have, shall we say, a strong interest in Mr. Somerton yourself. Am I to assume that these words mean nothing more than wishes, on your part?"

Pamela ignored the questions and repeated

her own. "Does the notion of such discord displease you, Mr. Henrick?"

Smoothly he replied, "Your Grace, my daughter's happiness is—must be—my greatest desire. If this marriage was indeed a mistake, then I must be very sorry for it. But I am not the sort of man to condemn a man and wife to stay chained to each other if misery is the result. I should sooner choose to take Elisabeth back home to live with me."

Pamela's own eyes had narrowed at this speech. "Then you would intervene, if you could?"

"If there was a need," he agreed.

With a sigh, the duchess leaned back. Her face gave no hint of the swiftness with which her mind raced forward. Languidly she replied, "As you must have guessed, Mr. Henrick, I am indeed concerned about your daughter as well as about Mr. Somerton. She is rather . . . unusual, quite out of the common way."

"She's always had an odd kick to her gallop," Henrick agreed tightly.

The duchess inclined her head graciously and continued, "As you say. But Darnell—Mr. Somerton is a most . . . conventional gentleman and I cannot believe he will be other than distressed by her eccentricities. Then I fear for her happiness. As I have good reason to know, Mr. Somerton has the devil's own temper when aroused, and an inability to countenance anything that smacks too bluntly of impropriety."

Henrick's eyebrows rose. "My Elisabeth has been indiscreet?" he asked with patent disbelief.

The duchess quickly recovered herself. Rather

crossly she said, "Well, no, but there must be some trouble between the two. I cannot believe they are suited as a pair."

In disgust John Henrick rose to his feet. "In short," he said bluntly, "this is all a tissue of suspicion and hope with nothing, whatsoever, of substance behind your words! As for Elisabeth, she would no more countenance impropriety than he would."

Sitting abruptly upright, the duchess demanded, "Do you mean she would not even countenance an ordinary affair on his part?"

"I do. But if the tattle-boxes are to be believed, Mr. Somerton is unlikely to indulge himself in one," was the acid reply.

Hastily Pamela rose to her feet and forced a smile. "Of course. How absurd of me to believe otherwise. But I had not realised you were on such excellent terms with your daughter and her husband. You were not, after all, at their wedding."

Henrick could cheerfully have strangled the duchess. Instead, he bowed and said grimly, "Pressing business kept me away."

"Of course," she replied soothingly. "No doubt you have, or soon will, call upon your son-in-law?"

Henrick bowed but did not answer. He seethed with fury, however, that Elisabeth had placed him in such a position. Reading aright the expression on Henrick's face, Pamela held out a hand and said, smoothly, "I shan't keep you any longer, then. But please—should you need my help—that is, discover that your daughter's match was not a felicitous one—I should be happy to help in any way I could."

Briefly Henrick took the proffered hand. "Thank you, your Grace," he said dryly.

Pamela rang for the footman to show Henrick out, and as soon as he was gone, she slammed the arm of her sofa in frustration. There must be a way to thrust the pair apart!

—13—

The Duchess of Carston need not have worried. Her words had given John Henrick a great deal to think about and it was not long before he did, indeed, call upon his son-in-law.

Darnell was in the library when Henrick was announced. Rather surprised, he told the footman, "Show him in here."

Somerton had very little time to wait. His first impression of Henrick was a surprisingly favourable one. A man of careless fashion, scarcely a dandy, and trim, although one would not expect to find him at an establishment such as Gentleman Jackson's. By reputation he was, moreover, a tolerable if not expert judge of horseflesh.

John Henrick was equally impressed with what he saw. True, this townhouse belonged to Viscount Langston, and not the man standing before him, but Somerton was the heir and it would be his soon enough. The dark oak shelves of the library filled with finely bound volumes, the Belgian carpets on the floor, the heavy satin draperies of dark green, and the massive mantel over the fireplace all bespoke generations of wealth and respectability. As for Somerton himself, Henrick saw a tall man with short, dark curls that were not in the least effeminate. The set of his jaws and the strength in his shoulders, moreover, removed any charge of dandyism the exquisite cut of his clothing might have suggested. It might have been expected that such a favourable impression would have warmed the heart of a doting father. Instead, John Henrick found himself beginning to hate the man before him. None of this showed in his face, however, as he stepped forward, bowed slightly, and extended a hand, "My son-in-law, I believe. I am delighted to meet you at last."

Darnell smiled with a charm that few women or men could resist. "And, sir, I am pleased to meet you."

Henrick coughed. "Yes. Well, if you had not married my daughter in such haste, I should have been at the wedding."

Somerton waved his father-in-law to a seat and offered him some port. When that was poured and both gentlemen comfortable, Darnell replied quietly, "You must forgive my devilish impatience, sir, but I have not regretted it."

A trifle severely, Henrick retorted, "Perhaps not. But have you considered the gossip it caused? There wasn't anything havey-cavey to the business, was there? Ain't breeding, is she?"

"No, there was not," Somerton said, setting down his glass with a distinct snap. "I should think you would know your daughter better than to ask such a question."

It was in that moment that inspiration struck and John Henrick saw clear the way to revenge himself upon his Elisabeth. Smoothly he set down his own glass of port and said, "Frankly, I came here to discuss marriage settlements with you, since I understand that matter was neglected in your haste to wed. But since we have been diverted, let us speak with no holds barred. I asked the question I did because I do, indeed, know my daughter, Elisabeth." He paused and held up a hand, "Before you take snuff at me, Mr. Somerton, I advise you to hear me out and consider carefully what I have to say. You appear to be in love with my daughter. A natural enough state of affairs. If she returns your affection, I must count you a very fortunate and very unusual fellow."

Darnell stared at his father-in-law, his impatience held tightly in check. But all he said was, "Go on."

Henrick looked down at his well-manicured nails and the pain was evident in his voice as he said, "I cannot like to tell you about Elisabeth, but I must. Had you come to me, before, and asked for her hand in marriage, I must have felt in duty bound to do so. Can you honestly say that it was not at her request that you failed to do so and that it was not at her request that the ceremony was performed with such unseemly haste?"

He paused and found, to his satisfaction, that Darnell could not answer him. He sighed and went on, "First, I must tell you some family history, shocking history. It is well-known that my father was fond of the muslin set. Well, one of these women approached my father and told him she carried his child. To his credit, he felt the need to make provision for her care, particularly when the mother died in childbirth. Unfortunately my father's choice was to raise the baby in his own household as though it were legitimate. The child's name was Letitia Roxbury, and to be fair, he never hid from her the circumstances of her birth. At any rate, she lived with us until my father's death, by which time she was notorious in the local countryside. Indeed, you may have heard of her, for she currently resides in London and is known as La Perdita."

"I cannot fathom what this has to do with Elisabeth," Somerton replied, somewhat less than politely.

Sorrow edged Henrick's voice as he said, "I blame myself. Elisabeth was too much in Letty's company as a child. We did, indeed, send her off to school, but by then it was too late." He paused and bit his lower lip. "You have, perhaps, wondered why Elisabeth was not brought out sooner. Well, I tell you frankly, Somerton, that, had I had my way, she would never have been brought out at all. In good conscience I could not have let any man marry her blindly, and who would have married her knowing her history?"

He paused and looked at Somerton, who replied impatiently, "Good God, sir! If you mean her aunt is an irrevocable barrier to marriage, you are much mistaken. No one could hold her liable for your father's actions."

Henrick sadly shook his head. "If it were only that! No, you do not know the half of it. My dearest Elisabeth! In the years between school and the time when she slipped away to London for this, her first Season, there were men. So many men, past counting even. I blush to say it, but I cannot even be certain there was not a baby, cut short upon the way."

Quietly Somerton rose to his feet. "You are a

damned liar," he said coolly. "Our wedding
night is sufficient proof of that, for me."

Henrick shrugged and turned his right hand
palm-up. "A sponge, a little blood. These things
are easily arranged. And who better to teach
the child than my half-sister, Letty?"

"I do not believe you," Darnell told his father-
in-law bluntly.

"No?" Henrick raised an eyebrow in disbelief.
"You have never felt my Elisabeth to be . . .
unusual? Never felt there was something in her
past, secrets she kept from you? And in bed?
Is she as you expected her to be? Can you even
swear that she does not visit my half-sister?
Ever? Or—"

"Enough!" Darnell's voice cut short the
demands. "Elisabeth is my wife and I will not
hear you speak of her in such a manner! I can
scarcely wonder that she did not want you at
our wedding, did not want me to ask your
permission for it to take place at all."

"So it *was* her notion after all," Henrick said
with mock surprise. "You will not hear what I
have to say about my daughter. Very well. I
shall leave you to your thoughts. But ask yourself if a dislike of me was her reason alone for
such haste. And do not blame me if you dislike
the answer."

With that, Henrick was gone, choosing not to
allow Somerton time to ring for a footman to
show him out. Slowly, Darnell turned away
from the door of the library and picked up his
glass again. It was absurd nonsense Henrick
had spoken. Somerton knew, from the first
time he had kissed Miss Harriet Tremaine,
that she, and therefore Elisabeth, was innocent and inexperienced in even the lightest of

passionate flirtations. But he could not help wondering what her past did hold. For Darnell could not entirely dismiss from his mind memories of times Elisabeth had turned away from him and refused to talk about her past, shrugging off his questions with a laugh. Nor could he deny the shadows that seemed to dim her face sometimes, as though her eyes did, indeed, hide some dark secret from him. And, most simply, why had she begun the masquerade of Harriet Tremaine in the first place. Thus, it was a very quiet husband who greeted Elisabeth when she returned from her afternoon shopping expedition a scant half-hour later.

"You shan't believe the ravishing hat I found," she cried, greeting Darnell with a kiss on the cheek. "And gloves! Half the usual price and guaranteed straight from Paris! I'm so exhausted, and yet I've had such a delightful time!"

Rather perfunctorily Darnell returned the kiss. "I'm pleased for you," he said quietly.

Abruptly, Elisabeth sat down and looked at her husband. "What's amiss?" she asked, equally quietly.

"Nothing. You need not regard it," he replied, hastily turning away. Elisabeth studied his back, trying to guess the trouble, and after a moment, Darnell seemed to recover. He turned and faced her, a thoughtful look on his face. "Elisabeth, shall we stay home tonight? And talk? I sometimes feel we are still such strangers to each other."

With every part of herself, Elisabeth wanted to say yes. She was, if possible, more in love with Darnell than when she married him. And yet, something made her hesitate. "As you

wish," she said, "though we are promised to
Sally Jersey. For dinner. I cannot quite like to
cry off now."

Darnell smiled perfunctorily. "Of course not,"
he agreed. "It was just a notion, and I daresay
we will have other opportunities to talk. Do
you know," he said somewhat wryly, "I had
not thought you would be such a social success."

Elisabeth regarded her husband with no little concern. "Are . . . are you displeased?" she
asked. "I thought only to be a credit to you. We
shall not cry off tonight, but if you wish it, I
can plan otherwise, after this."

He hesitated, then shook his head and smiled.
"No, my dear, you need not do so on my
account." Darnell took her hands in his and
said, "Forgive me. I have had a most unpleasant afternoon—accounts and such. But it don't
signify. We shall go to Sally Jersey's affair and
I shall, indeed, be proud of you. Now, you'd
best go upstairs to dress or we shall be late!"

Elisabeth was not altogether satisfied with
this, but she dared not pursue it further.
Instead, without haste, she withdrew her hands
from his and reached up to draw Darnell's
face down to her own. Then slowly, deliberately,
she kissed him with a thoroughness she would
not have understood a few months before. The
crush of his arms about her, in response, made
her whisper, "It is not, I believe, unfashionable
to be late, sir. We could go upstairs to our
room together . . ."

"Baggage!" He laughed. Then, caressingly,
"You go ahead. I shall be up in a moment. And
tell your maid to go to the devil! *I* shall help
you dress."

With a gurgle of laughter, Elisabeth swept

out of the room. Alone, Darnell said aloud, "My dear father-in-law, Elisabeth is the dearest woman I have ever known, and I swear you shan't come between us!"

Then, tidying up one or two matters, Darnell Somerton followed his wife upstairs. They were, indeed, late to Sally Jersey's dinner party.

14

Elisabeth had no suspicion of her father's visit to Darnell. She knew, of course, that he was in London. Marietta had seen to that, informing Elisabeth, with a sniff, that it was all very well to dislike members of one's family, but one ought not to flaunt such disputes in public. "Well, I shall not cut him if our paths cross," Elisabeth said judiciously, "but I cannot bring myself to be on intimate terms with him."

Knowing her cousin to be headstrong, Marietta dropped the matter and Elisabeth thrust it to the back of her mind. Her only fear was an encounter between Darnell and her father, but she was certain he would have told her if this had occurred. He did not tell her, however. Precisely why he did not tell her, he could not have said. At first it was a dislike of distressing her, and after meeting John Henrick, Darnell understood very well why Elisabeth disliked her father. But as time passed, the seed Henrick had sown grew. Somerton did not believe the charge that Elisabeth had allowed a slip on the shoulder, but he could not help beginning to wonder if there were not, indeed, *some* truth to the matter. As for Elisabeth, she was far too happy to be afraid. And happiness made her more beautiful. Unfortunately, under the cir-

cumstances, beauty was not altogether a felicitous thing, for, as a wife, Elisabeth found herself more popular with the gentlemen than
ever. Before John Henrick's visit, Somerton
had delighted in his wife's success. But now it
gave him pause, and the first faint stirrings of
jealousy occurred. Perhaps it was this jealousy
that led to his kindness to the Duchess of
Carston at a garden party a week or two after
Henrick's visit.

"How delighted I am to see you!" Lady
Bromley told them effusively upon their arrival.
"Mrs. Somerton! Why, what a sly little puss
you are! You must know everyone was convinced Mr. Somerton would *never* marry. It
was quite the most delicious *on-dit* when one
heard he had! Someday you *must* tell me how
you did it."

"Yes, well, thank you," Darnell said, with a
politeness that was entirely feigned, "but please
excuse us, Lady Bromley. My wife is a trifle
overcome by the heat and I wish to fetch her
some lemonade." Without waiting for a reply,
he took a firm grip on Elisabeth's arm and
guided her ruthlessly towards a shaded portion of the garden.

As soon as they were out of earshot of Lady
Bromley, Elisabeth gave a gurgle of laughter
and said, "Overcome, indeed! What a bouncer."

Darnell looked at her with a smile. "Did you
mind?" he asked. "I quite thought you would
be happy to be rescued from that creature's
impertinence."

Elisabeth laughed again. "I was," she con-
fessed. "What an outrageous woman!"

Darnell shrugged. "Put her out of your mind,

then," he advised, "and look about you, instead, for someone you would like to see."

"The person I would like to see," Elisabeth told him frankly, "is your sister-in-law, Olivia. Where is she? She quite promised to stand by me, this afternoon."

"She will no doubt be along in her own good time," Darnell replied soothingly. "Olivia is scarcely ever on time for anything. But are you really in need of support today? And won't I do?" he asked, a faint frown creasing his handsome brow, "I had thought that was, in part, what husbands were for!"

Elisabeth looked up at him with a smile. "They are," she assured him warmly. "It is just that there are so many ... tattle-boxes here, today, and I trusted Olivia to see me through."

Somerton threw back his head and laughed. "My love, if they are cruel to you, it is only envy and you need only cut them. What can it matter what they think?"

It was, Elisabeth reflected wryly, impossible to explain to a man the importance such tattle-boxes carried with their gossip. So she only said, aloud, "Will you fetch me that glass of lemonade, Darry? I should like it, above all things, and then perhaps you can make me known to some of the people you know here."

"Of course. I shall be back soon," he said, favouring her with his warmest smile.

Unfortunately, it was some time before Somerton returned. As she waited, Elisabeth found herself hailed by a figure she had come to dread. "Hello, your Grace," Elisabeth said coolly.

The Duchess of Carston smiled, not in the least distressed by the lack of warmth in

Elisabeth's voice. Her own seemed almost to caress as she said, "My very dear Mrs. Somerton, how I have longed for the opportunity to speak with you alone! For you must know what very good friends your husband and I have been."

"Indeed?" The tone was not inviting.

"But of course! Hasn't he told you?" the duchess demanded with wide-eyed innocence. "For shame! Indeed, he offered for me, my first Season, and though I must blush to say so, I came close to eloping with him. My father, you see, would not countenance the match." Pamela paused with a sigh as she regarded Elisabeth from beneath long lashes. After a moment she went on, "Of course, during my first marriage Darry was so very discreet. But when I was widowed, we had no such need."

"And yet you are married to the Duke of Carston now, are you not?" Elisabeth pointed out dryly.

Pamela's eyes glittered a moment. Then with a laugh she said, "And so we are once again discreet! You mustn't, my dear, confuse marriage with passion or love. There are many reasons to marry, and none of them need interfere with one's pleasure."

Elisabeth stared at the duchess uncertainly. Her words did not fit with the Darnell she felt she knew. But she could not deny how often she had heard his name linked with that of the duchess when friends of his spoke of the past. Pamela was not oblivious to the stir she had caused in Elisabeth's breast. When she judged enough time had passed, she added, "If you wish to see the truth of what I say, then watch for when Darry shall take me off into the hedges. Follow us by five minutes and I warrant for the proof." And with a laugh she was gone.

Thus it was that Elisabeth looked around anxiously for Darnell and found, instead, Lord Harold Weatherby, one of her more persistent and more attractive admirers. This was the sight that greeted Somerton's eyes when he returned with the lemonade he had promised her. For the first time, Darnell felt himself truly jealous as he watched his friend's handsome face smiling at Elisabeth. To judge from her blushing laughter, Weatherby was paying her extravagant compliments and Elisabeth was more than a little pleased at his attention. Darnell did not trust himself to approach the couple, and abruptly, he turned on his heel and strode away in search of something—anything—to distract his mind from what he had just seen.

The Duchess of Carston watched with something akin to delight. She did not miss the darkness that crossed Somerton's face as he observed his wife and friend, and she determined to profit from it. Silently she followed him, and when he slipped away to a deserted portion of the garden, she followed, pausing only long enough to direct a footman to send Mrs. Elisabeth Somerton after them once a few minutes had passed. It was not precisely what she had planned, but it would do.

As for Darnell, he seemed scarcely surprised to see the duchess.

"Darry!" she called out after him, causing him to stop and turn to face her. "Darry, how pleased I am to see you," she said, a trifle breathlessly, as she caught up with him. "Where is your lovely wife?" His face darkened again and she made haste to say, "I have wanted, for some time, Darry, to have the chance to wish you well, and to tell you how happy I am that you have found someone to love. I presume it *was* love, and not a marriage of convenience?"

"It was," Darnell said shortly.

He did not smile, however, and Pamela took his arm. "You don't believe me," she scolded him, "but I truly am happy for you. However selfish you may think me, I genuinely do wish for you to find contentment."

Even Somerton was not impervious to her charm. His face softened as he said, "Thank you, Pamela. I do believe you and am grateful to you for your good wishes. If . . . if I have been unkind to *you*, please try to understand. I will not cuckold another man's wife."

"I do understand," she assured him warmly. "And honour you for your sentiments, however much they may come between us." She stopped and turned liquid blue eyes up at him. "Darry," she said softly, "will you just kiss me once? For the sake of the love we might once have shared?"

Without speaking, Somerton took her in his arms and gently, but thoroughly kissed her. It was, for both of them, a magical sort of moment and seemed never to end. Never, that is, until a sharp gasp thrust them back into the present. As one, they turned to look and found Elisabeth staring at them, her hand covering her mouth, eyes wide with hurt betrayal. Before either could speak, she was gone, turning on her heel and running down a path, heedless of the picture she made, wanting only to get away.

"Damme!" he exclaimed under his breath, at once letting go of the duchess. "Elisabeth!"

Pamela watched him go, unable to hide the triumph in her eyes. And, indeed, there was no need.

As for Elisabeth, she ran through the grounds of Lady Bromley's estate, stopping only when she ran headlong into someone's arms. "Forgive me," she said hastily, and tried to pull free.

But she could not. And when Elisabeth looked up, she discovered that her captor was John Henrick, her father. "Well, well," he said, with a smile that chilled her. "What is my hoyden running from, this time? Not, I trust, some tattle-box? Or gentleman you imagine has thrust himself upon you? Perhaps it is your perfect husband?" Elisabeth was unable to hide her start at these last words and Henrick whistled. "So it *is* your husband! I told you, my dear, you would not find marriage the joy you thought it to be. And what has he done now? Or what do you *imagine* he has done?"

Abruptly Elisabeth pulled free. "Stop it!" she cried. "I will not listen to your poison."

"Poison?" Henrick raised his eyebrows. "When I want only what is best for you?"

Elisabeth had no chance to reply, for at that moment Darnell discovered them. "Elisabeth," he said anxiously. Then, "Mr. Henrick, I did not realise you were here."

Henrick bowed. "I have been trying to understand what it is that so overset my dear Elisabeth."

She looked away and he flushed. "A misunderstanding," Darnell said briefly.

"I think not," Elisabeth said in a voice that was steadier than she would have expected.

"It was," he answered, meeting her eyes and holding them.

Elisabeth was the first to look away, a fact not lost on Henrick. With an inner smile he said, smoothly, "Whatever has occurred, I suggest it would be better to settle the matter when you are once more alone. Your prolonged absence will not have escaped notice, and while it is all very well to speak of love matches, it is still bad *ton* to disappear at a party."

"You are right," Somerton agreed, collecting himself with great effort. "Elisabeth, shall we go and see if Olivia has arrived?"

She nodded and forced herself to take his arm. Again Henrick smiled, then said, deprecatingly, "Perhaps I might accompany you? If the gossips then choose to comment upon your absence, they must also note that I was with you *and that we are on the best of terms.*"

Reluctantly, Darnell said, "Very well, sir. And . . . thank you."

Henrick merely bowed. Elisabeth dug her fingers deeper into Somerton's arm and leaned closer, a circumstance that only increased Darnell's discomfort. To everyone's (except perhaps John Henrick's) relief, Olivia and Robert Somerton were soon found. Henrick contrived to have himself presented and then took his leave of the group. Only Elisabeth heard his whispered words, "You are my daughter and I *shall* have you back!"

Olivia was all concern. "Elisabeth! You are positively pale! Are you unwell?" Then, as a rather indelicate thought occurred to her, she lowered her voice and asked, in a conspirator's voice, "You are not breeding, are you?"

Elisabeth was very grateful that she could say, with perfect truth, "I am not."

"Oh, well, don't be discouraged; you will be soon enough," Olivia replied consolingly.

Elisabeth could not entirely suppress a smile at the disappointment patent in Olivia's face. She turned a light reply, however, and they were soon thoroughly engrossed in the party. If Elisabeth continued to feel strained and as though a heavy lump had settled inside her, she allowed none of it to show. Indeed, more than one member of the *ton* was heard to remark grudgingly upon her pretty manners. Only Somerton might have guessed how she felt, and he was too preoccupied with the role he played, as gracious guest, to say so.

Later, as the party rode back to town in the Somerton coach, Elisabeth had time to think. Particularly about her encounter with her father, for she was determined not to dwell upon the scene with the duchess. And as she thought about the matter, it occurred to Elisabeth that one might, from their manner, have concluded that Darnell and her father were already acquainted. She had been too distressed, at the time, to notice, but in retrospect the fact was marked.

Darnell, watching his wife from the opposite corner of the carriage, bleakly noted the changes on her face as she considered the events of the party. He was not looking forward to the discussion that he knew must soon follow. And Olivia watched both of them, a small smile upon her face. Lord, but seeing Darry married was far more amusing than she had expected it would be!

* * *

She was not, Elisabeth reminded herself sternly, a coward. It was therefore that same evening that she asked Darnell to accompany her upstairs early, ignoring the knowing glances of the rest of the family. Curtly he agreed and followed scarcely two paces behind. Elisabeth was intolerably aware of how close he was and how much she wanted him in spite of what the duchess had told her and in spite of what she had seen. Perhaps it was his courage that failed, for at the door of their room he said, "Let us undress and then we may talk as long as you wish."

"I wish to talk *now*," she retorted evenly.

Wryly he smiled at her. "Well, I do not. Not until I have released my neck from this devilishly tight cravat and changed to something far more comfortable than the knee breeches my father prefers as evening dress." She did not answer and he tried to jest with her. "You are wondering, of course, why we continue to live here if I dislike the custom so much. Well, I had not meant to tell you quite yet, but I have taken a house for us. It is to be ready very shortly. And while it is only a furnished place I have arranged for, at present, I mean for us to be comfortable there. Do you like the notion?"

Elisabeth's face lit up. "Oh, yes!" Then, as she recalled what had occurred, she sobered and said, somewhat stiffly, "We have, nevertheless, other matters to speak of."

Somerton bowed politely. "I shall join you shortly. But now Grant, my valet, is awaiting me in my dressing room."

There was nothing to say to that, and as Elisabeth watched Darnell enter his dressing room, she felt that miles, rather than one wall,

separated them. Her own maid was waiting to
help her undress, and she made no demur.
Instead, Elisabeth pondered the news Darnell
had just given her. It was true she often wished
they might have a place of their own, but she
could scarcely ask him to purchase one when
he was the heir and this townhouse would be
his soon enough. Particularly as it was unlikely the viscount and his wife would, in
general, spend so much time in London as they
had this Season. It was simply one more piece
of the puzzle that was her husband. Quietly
she allowed herself to be undressed. Then,
clad in her nightshift, Elisabeth dismissed her
maid, for she wanted no interested ears about
when she confronted Darnell about the Duchess of Carston.

Thus it was that Darnell found her sitting
in front of her mirror, slowly brushing out her
long chestnut hair. He reached out, without
thinking, to touch her. With the first touch of
his fingers, Elisabeth shivered and turned to
look up at Darnell. He was dressed in a robe of
wine satin that lent fire to his eyes, and she
could think of nothing but what lay under that
robe. Slowly she rose and stood before him in a
nightshift scarcely more concealing than the
one she had worn on her wedding night. And
suddenly nothing mattered but that she was his
wife. "Oh, Darry," she whispered, reaching
out for him.

Somerton answered not with words but with
a mouth and tongue that greeted hers hungrily,
wanting everything she could give. Elisabeth
shivered again and this time her hands did
reach inside his robe, seeking the familiar places
that had become so dear to her. And it was

Darnell's turn to moan. With a rashness so like him, he tugged at her shift and, when it would not yield, tore it in one horrendous pull, to leave Elisabeth bare before him. And then his hands were the ones who searched and stroked and roused her fires. Moments later they were on the bed, neither quite knew how, and Darnell cast off his dressing gown with a curse. "Blasted thing, I shall have to burn it!" he muttered as he struggled with it.

Elisabeth made no effort to hide her laughter.

"So that's the way it is, is it?" he growled. "Then you deserve a lesson for laughing so disrespectfully!"

As Elisabeth laughed again and struggled to pull away from him, Darnell pinned her easily and lay half his weight upon her, holding her hands about her head. Then slowly, tantalisingly, he lowered his head to kiss her, softly, then demandingly. With practised ease, he edged her thighs apart with his knee. And then waited. Elisabeth's eyes widened as she realised what he was about, and without knowing it, her back arched toward him. He gave a triumphant crow of laughter and swooped down on her, his hands once more free to explore the body that lay below him. Her hands were equally eager, and soon, one in their urgent need, they crested, clinging to each other as if there were no reality but this.

Later, as she lay in the crook of his arm, Elisabeth said quietly, "What happened this afternoon, Darry?"

Even before he spoke, she felt him stiffen. "I kissed her Grace, the Duchess of Carston," he said curtly. "I wanted to and I did."

Slowly, painfully, Elisabeth digested this

reply. "I see," she said at last. "I suppose I was not to know about it?"

"You were not," he confirmed.

For some long moments, Elisabeth lay in silence, wondering what she could say to this man who was her husband and who had suddenly become a stranger. He had never promised her fidelity, but then she had been so sure of him that she had never thought to ask it. And that brought the unwelcome reminder that she was scarcely someone able to chastise him for his behaviour. She had, after all, married him, in part, to escape her father. That she loved him seemed not sufficient an excuse for leg-shackling him without first telling him the truth of her past. Nevertheless, she could not keep herself from asking, "Will it happen again?"

"It may," he retorted as bluntly as ever. A sharp cry escaped her and his voice became more brutal than ever. "I remind you," he said, "that I told you on our wedding day that it should be pound dealings only, that I should always be honest with you."

Elisabeth laughed shortly. "Indeed?" she said. "Then why did you never tell me you had met my father? Before today, I mean?" She turned and looked up at Darnell, propping herself on one elbow.

Anger filled his eyes and his voice was grim as he replied, "I had not thought to face a Spanish Inquisition tonight, madam. Nor is it something I will tolerate. If you wish to know of my dealings with your father, ask him," he added cruelly.

"I shall!" she flung back at him, knowing it to be an empty threat.

For a moment, they stared at each other, eyes flashing. Then, abruptly, Darnell pulled free and out of bed. "Where are you going?" Elisabeth cried.

Deliberately he looked at her. "I don't know. Rest assured, however, that I shall not disturb you again tonight."

And then he was gone, leaving Elisabeth to stare, mouth gaping open, after him.

—15—

An uneasy truce settled between Elisabeth and
Darnell. If it was guilt that had led Somerton
to be so curt with her, it was now pride that
kept Elisabeth from raising the subject again.
More than once Darnell found himself asking:
Why the devil had Elisabeth followed him at
the party? And why the devil had Pamela
chosen to kiss him just when she did? And if
Darnell had pushed to the back of his mind
the charges Henrick had laid against his daughter, she could not help but wonder what they
might have been. For Elisabeth could not believe her father had said nothing to Darnell,
but fear kept her from asking.

Not even the prospect of moving into the
house he had hired could help. And yet, when
the time came to do so, a week after their
quarrel, Elisabeth could not conceal her pleasure at the sight of the neat little house in a
fashionable section of London. The servants
were hired and waiting when they arrived,
and Elisabeth's maid and Darnell's valet followed with their belongings. It was, in short,
an easy affair to be accomplished. Even the
viscount and his wife seemed to approve the
move. "A wise notion, I should think," Lord

Langston had said, upon being informed of their plans.

"Yes. Particularly as we shall be staying some while longer here," Darnell's mother had added. "I find I rather like London, just now."

If there had been envy in Olivia's eyes, she did not say so, but wished her brother-in-law and his wife well.

With a kind of grave courtesy Darnell escorted his wife inside their new home and introduced her to the servants. "Philip interviewed them for us," he explained quietly in advance. "But you need not retain any you dislike." He hesitated, then went on, "Tomorrow we shall settle upon an allowance for household needs. And decide if there are any changes you wish to make in the furnishings."

Elisabeth nodded, not trusting herself to speak. She was, however, all courtesy when she greeted her staff, taking a liking immediately to the housekeeper. It seemed to her an extravagance to hire someone to manage the household when she was perfectly capable of doing so herself, but Darnell only said, when asked about it, "I wish you to have time to do the things you wish to do."

And if I wish to be busy? Elisabeth asked herself silently. But she could not bring herself to tell him that she was not suited to a life of leisure, for that would have meant telling him about Harriet Tremaine. Instead, she began to spend much of her free time accompanying Lady Langston on her visits to schools and hospitals in the poorer sections of London. If Darnell approved or disapproved, he never said so and Elisabeth was left with the lowering reflection that perhaps it was because he simply didn't care.

As for Darnell, he found himself spending much of his time at his clubs and, increasingly, lost in thought. Indeed, upon one such occasion Darnell was so intent upon his thoughts that he scarcely heard Sir Peter Dunsworth hailing him. "Darry! Splendid to see you! Where are you off to?"

On perhaps the third try, Sir Peter succeeded in capturing Somerton's attention. "Sorry," Darnell said curtly. "I was wool-gathering. How are you, Peter?"

Dunsworth eyed his friend warily. "Well, enough," he answered. "Point is, how are *you*?" When Darnell did not answer, Sir Peter nodded. "Aye, that's the way of it. A quarrel. Knew it would come to that. Always does. Suppose that means you'll spend the day all Friday-faced and sighing."

In spite of himself, Darnell threw back his head and laughed. As Sir Peter eyed him aggrievedly, Somerton made haste to say, "You are the one with the Friday-face, you know."

"Now, now, that won't do," Sir Peter told his friend severely. "Won't have you bamming me. Meant to ask you if you wished to look in at Tattersall's, but not if you intend to be walking about all day lost in your thoughts."

"I shan't be," Somerton promised with a laugh. "What are you looking for? A pair?"

"Aye. Stanhope's breakdowns. Means to offer them for sale, today, if what I've heard is true." A thought occurred to Sir Peter and he stopped to stare morosely at Darnell. "Unless you mean to bid against me?"

Darnell shook his head. "Too showy, by half,

for me. Particularly as I've told you before that I expect them to throw out a splint at the first point they are pressed for speed."

"No such thing!" Sir Peter retorted angrily.

Unwilling to argue the matter, Somerton shrugged. "In any event, I am content with my own stable."

Sir Peter frowned. "What about your wife? Haven't seen her on a horse yet. Told me she was devilish fond of riding."

"She told me that once, herself," Somerton said slowly, "but I had forgotten."

"What I want to know is why I haven't seen her out riding, then," Sir Peter persisted.

"Because she hasn't a horse to ride!" Darnell retorted with exasperation.

Sir Peter shook his head gravely. "Very bad form. Ought to buy her one."

"Thank you," Darnell said in a voice heavy with sarcasm. "I have already made up my mind to do so."

"Good," Sir Peter said with patent approval. "There's a nice mare due to be put up for sale today. Heard Sally Jersey wanted her, but she might give way for you."

"And she may not," Somerton retorted.

"True," Sir Peter conceded graciously. "But if so, we shall come about. Any number of horses to be had, just now. Are you *sure* you don't want a pair?"

Sir Peter and Darnell were not the only ones to have taken the notion to visit Tattersall's. Robert Somerton was also there as well as any number of other male members of the *ton*. There were very few females and those present drew disapproving stares, for Tattersall's was generally accounted a male preserve. All, that is,

save Letitia Roxbury—La Perdita. She was, as
always, the centre of flattering attention, having come, as she cheerfully informed those who
asked, to bid for a pair for her new high-perch
phaeton. "There's your competition for Stanhope's breakdowns," Darnell told Sir Peter,
indicating Letitia Roxbury and the gossip cir-
culating about her.

Dunsworth sighed. "Worst part of it is," he
confided, "I shan't regret it if she does get 'em.
Sort of woman La Perdita is. One *wants* to do
things for her."

Remembering John Henrick's words, Darnell
studied his wife's celebrated relative. He had
seen her before, of course, but never with the
need to know what she was like. As he stared,
Letitia Roxbury turned and her eyes met his.
Very deliberately she returned his stare and,
finally, nodded graciously to him. Amused by
her presumption, for Darnell was certain she
had guessed or knew who he was, he bowed
slightly. As though it had been a signal, Letitia
quietly but effectively detached herself from
the group of gentlemen that surrounded her.
Without haste, so that he might have time to
escape if he chose, she approached Darnell.
When she was quite close, she held out a hand,
and with the briefest of hesitation he took it.
"Mr. Darnell Somerton, I presume?"

He bowed. "La Perdita, of course."

She inclined her head and said quietly, "We
have, I believe, a mutual interest?"

Sir Peter shook his head. "No, you don't.
Darry ain't bidding on the pair. I am!"

La Perdita included Sir Peter in her smile.
"I must have been misinformed. How high do
you intend to go, sir?"

For several minutes the talk was of horses, but Somerton was not deceived. He was certain that Letitia Roxbury was studying him—for what purpose, he was unsure. If it was because of Elisabeth, her audacity and impertinence were intolerable, and yet, what other reason could there be? Did she truly wish to risk her niece's reputation so carelessly? As he considered the matter, Darnell began to feel angry on Elisabeth's behalf. It would not help her position if her connection with Letitia Roxbury became the latest *on-dit*. But Letitia, it seemed, was all discretion, after all. She did not mention Elisabeth, but rather spoke of other matters, including a reference to his father, the viscount, with whom it seemed she had a slight acquaintance. Which would, Darnell thought, neatly explain her desire to speak with him and distract attention from her relationship to Elisabeth. His respect for La Perdita grew accordingly.

And then she withdrew, pausing only long enough to once again extend a hand to Darnell and express the hope that they might meet again. All very discreet. As she walked away, Robert Somerton joined them. "I say, was that La Perdita?" he asked in astonishment.

Sir Peter nodded. "Wishes to bid for the pair and heard one of us meant to, as well. Hoped to charm us into giving way for her."

Robert looked at Darnell, who added quietly, "It also appears she has a slight acquaintance with Father."

The younger Somerton raised his eyebrows in surprise. "Does she now? Dashed bold-faced of her to say so!"

Darnell smiled. "She did not indicate there

was anything improper involved. Indeed, I think it had to do with a chance encounter through a friend of his who was involved with her, at the time."

Robert did not seem entirely mollified, but he had no opportunity to pursue the matter. Sir Peter had become impatient, and he said, a trifle petulantly, "That's all very well for you to stand there talking family matters, but I've come to look at horses!"

"I beg your pardon," Darnell said gravely.

"I came to meet Weathersham," Robert said. "Have you seen him? I intend to wangle an invitation to go hunting in the shires in the fall."

"Saw him earlier," Sir Peter said helpfully. "Wanted to look at a rather nice gelding offered for sale. Might look for him over there."

Robert Somerton looked in the direction Sir Peter indicated. "Thank you," he said. "And you'll excuse me, I know. I shall look in on you sometime soon, Darry," he said. "Haven't really seen your new house yet, you know."

"New house?" Sir Peter looked at his friend somewhat aggrievedly.

Darnell smiled. "The family townhouse had, er, become a trifle crowded," he explained. "So I've hired a place for Elisabeth and myself."

"Dashed sensible!" Dunsworth pronounced approvingly. "Don't like to say it, but wouldn't be able to abide sharing a house with my relatives. If one ain't matchmaking or asking about one's gaming, another is. And if one's a female, it's worse! M'in-laws are forever asking m'sister if she's breeding yet. Intolerable!"

Darnell hid a smile and neatly turned the subject. "Why, Dunsworth, are we still stand-

ing here? I thought," he said coolly, "that you
wanted to look at horses?"

"I do. And no more time wasted, either!"

It was rather late, that afternoon, when
Somerton returned home, and he had difficulty restraining his impatience upon learning
that Elisabeth was still out. The mare was not
to be delivered until later, but in buying her,
Darnell had discovered in himself a desire to
have some time with Elisabeth alone again.
The distance between them seemed intolerable
and he wanted to talk with her, regain the
closeness. As it was, however, Darnell directed
the footman to inform him directly Mrs. Somerton returned, and he paced about the library,
conscious of the time they had lost.

In the end, Darnell received a summons not
only to greet Elisabeth, but to take charge of
the mare, for they arrived at the same moment.
He hurried out onto the front steps and found
Elisabeth stroking the mare's mane and saying,
"What a lovely horse! Whoever can she belong
to?"

"You." Darnell's voice came from directly
behind Elisabeth, and she turned with a start.
To her surprise, he smiled and said, "I remembered that you once said you loved to ride. I
thought you might like a mare for use here in
London. Do you like her?"

Elisabeth let go of the mare and, heedless of
the picture she made, threw her arms around
Darnell's neck. "Oh, yes," she cried.

The groom delivering the horse coughed
discreetly, and Somerton gently set aside his
wife. "Thank you," he told the fellow gravely.
"If you will wait a moment, I shall have my

own groom come round and take charge of her for you."

But there was no need to do so. Philip had selected the staff for Darnell's new house most carefully, and the alert footman had immediately sent to the kitchen for the groom that was waiting there. So by the time Darnell turned round towards the house, Tom, the groom, was already coming towards them. The necessary orders were given, and within a few minutes, Darnell and Elisabeth were able to proceed inside. Somerton noted the flushed pleasure on her face and realised that he had not seen her smile so fully since the night of their argument. Without realising he had done so, Darnell invited her to join him in the library and tell him where she had been. Elisabeth was not one to spurn the first overture in some days and she happily told him about her mother-in-law's newest charity.

Later, as they lay in bed together, Darnell asked, "Why didn't you remind me that you would have liked a horse to ride? You need only have asked."

Elisabeth hesitated. "You have already given me so much and I did not like to ask for more."

Darnell took her hands in his. "You shall always have all that you wish—I swear it. And you must never fear to ask again."

To his surprise, Elisabeth hesitated. Then she said, "I am not altogether sure I should like to have everything so easily. Sometimes I fear myself becoming like some ladies I have seen: all thoughts of clothes and possessions and nothing else to live for. To be sure, it is pleasant to be able to have the things I wish, and not to need fear being poor. But it is as well to pause, sometimes, and not have this or that trifle."

Puzzled, Darnell said, "You seem in a most somber mood tonight, love."

She smiled fleetingly. "When I go with your mother, I am always reminded how easily it might have been I needing help rather than offering it."

"Don't go, then," he answered promptly.

"How can I not go?" Elisabeth asked quietly. "I have so much and they so little. Moreover, I know what it is to be alone and desperate."

Carefully, not wishing to frighten her, Darnell said, "How do you know that?"

Elisabeth looked at him, her eyes frightened ovals. Anxiously they tried to read the question in his. Stammering, she said, "I . . . I cannot speak of it. Not yet. Please do not press me on this."

Darnell continued to hold her gaze, levelly, for several moments. Though her eyes unmistakably held fear, she did not waver. Finally he said, "When and where you will, love."

He kissed her, then, and the kiss led to a caress and something more. The joy they felt in each other's bodies was still too new to seem permanent, and they treasured each reassurance of it. So, for the third time that night, Darnell and Elisabeth made love.

—16—

Elisabeth was eager to put the mare through her paces and she set off for the park early the next morning. Darnell declined to accompany her, pleading business with his solicitor. "But I shall try to join you after a short while," he told Elisabeth as he helped her mount her horse.

"Good, I shall look for you," she told him cheerfully.

Then Elisabeth was off, keeping an easy check on the restless mare. "I know," she said consolingly. "I should like a good gallop as much as you. But we are in London now and must behave like ladies!" As if in sympathy, the mare whinnied, and Elisabeth laughed happily.

The day was a pleasant one, the cooler weather having already begun to set in. Overhead, a few clouds rolled by and in the park the grass showed evidence of being pleased by the recent rain. It was soon evident that a good many other members of the *ton* were also out and about enjoying the weather, including Lord Harold Weatherby. "I say! Mrs. Somerton! Elisabeth! Wait up a moment!" he hailed her.

Startled, Elisabeth looked about, then espied Weatherby. With a friendly smile she reined in her mare and replied, "Lord Weatherby, how delightful to see you. I am afraid Darry could not accompany me, this morning, but you will find him if you take a look-in at the house."

Weatherby smiled and said, gallantly, "Darry may go to the devil, for all I care. I am satisfied to have the opportunity to ride with you."

Elisabeth frowned slightly. She knew that such extravagant compliments were fashionable, but as always, they made her a trifle uneasy. Nevertheless, she replied lightly, "No Spanish coin, my Lord. I am feeling far too wise to be deceived by such, this fine morning."

Lord Weatherby gave a mock sigh. "Alas, you have crushed my dearest hopes! I shall go out and shoot myself."

In spite of herself, Elisabeth laughed. "Do give over such nonsense, Harry! You know very well you like my company solely because you need not fear I am setting my cap at you."

Lord Weatherby's eyes twinkled as he replied, "There is a great deal in what you say, of course. Still, I should not say that was *solely* the reason. You do have a way of making a man feel at ease with you. One needn't feel one is expected to do the pretty to you all the time."

It was Elisabeth's turn to roast him. "But, Lord Weatherby," she answered a trifle breathlessly, "you do the pretty so well!"

Weatherby sighed again. "But, you see, that is precisely the problem. I find myself charming the girl, quite without intending to, and the next thing I know, her mother is hinting they expect me to offer for her! Man can't live that way."

"Poor Weatherby, a sad case, indeed," Elisabeth said soothingly.

"Aye, and what's the remedy?" he demanded in return.

A mischievous look crept into Elisabeth's eyes, and it was with great difficulty that she kept her voice grave as she replied, "I can see only one thing for it, Harry."

"What?" he asked eagerly.

She turned wide, innocent eyes on him. "Why, marry, of course! Then all the girls will cease to set their caps at you."

For a moment Weatherby was silent, his eyes bulging in astonishment. Then he recovered himself, but before he could speak, Elisabeth laughed and urged her mare to gallop away from him. With no thought to their appearance, Weatherby pursued her, catching up with Elisabeth's mare only at the end of the lane. There, together, the pair unabashedly laughed helplessly together. Unfortunately, it was at precisely this moment that Darnell reached them, having been afforded an excellent view of the entire race. Elisabeth espied him first and cried out, "Darry! You came! I did not expect you so soon."

"That seems quite evident," Somerton replied coldly.

"I say," Weatherby broke in with a frown, "you're in the devil's own mood, Darry. What's put the wind up in you?"

Somerton turned a quelling stare on his friend. "The sight of my wife galloping through the park like any heedless hoyden has set my mood. Must the two of you make such a spectacle of yourselves?"

"No, dash it, Darry! That's going too far," Weatherby protested.

"Is it?" Darnell demanded, turning to Elisabeth. "Look at my wife. Her hairpins must be scattered all up and down the path."

Elisabeth regarded Darnell steadily, for a moment, then said quietly, "No doubt you are right, Darry, in saying that we were imprudent. But that is all. The matter is best forgotten. Unless you wish to make a further spectacle of us with your angry scolding?"

Somerton's eyes narrowed, but he said, curtly, "Very well. We shall discuss this again when we are in private, Elisabeth."

Relieved, Weatherby said, "Aye, that's the ticket. Well, must be off. Good day, Darry. Mrs. Somerton."

They murmured a farewell in return and watched him go. Then Darnell turned to his wife and said, as they urged their horses to a decorous pace, "Must you encourage that fellow, Elisabeth?"

She turned puzzled eyes on him. "Isn't Lord Weatherby a friend of yours?" she asked. "Do you wish me to cut him?"

"Of course not!" Somerton retorted in exasperation. "But there is no need to encourage the fellow to dangle about you. It don't look right."

Elisabeth's eyes narrowed, but she determined to return a soft answer. "I shall discourage Harry, if you dislike it so much."

"*Harry?*" Somerton thundered. "You call him Harry?"

Her temper began to rise. "Why not?" she asked quietly. "He is an old friend of yours and you do not object when I call Dunsworth Peter."

"It is not the same thing," Darnell said stoutly.

"Why not?"

"Because Peter is not always hanging about, making calves eyes at you," Darnell retorted, goaded beyond endurance.

All hope of restraint was gone, and Letty would have recognised the dangerous gleam in Elisabeth's eyes. "Indeed?" she asked. "And what of your friend, the Duchess of Carston? Am I allowed to object that you call her Pamela?"

"That is another matter, altogether."

Elisabeth faced her husband, rigid with anger. In measured tones she said, "Is it? Well, I shall pay precisely as much attention to your wishes concerning Lord Weatherby—or any other gentleman—as you do to mine concerning her Grace."

Their eyes locked and neither gave way until an angry voice intruded. "Look out there, you're blocking the entire path."

Hastily Darnell and Elisabeth moved out of the way of the offended party of riders. As they did so, Elisabeth looked about for a way to impress her determination on Darnell. She saw it in Letty. La Perdita had not outbid Dunsworth for Stanhope's pair, but she had found a pretty little mare and was riding it in the park this morning with a gentleman Elisabeth recognised as a frequent visitor to her aunt's.

Elisabeth had no real intention of jeopardising her reputation by speaking with Letty in such a public place, but she did wish to shock Darnell. It was foolish and imprudent, and that is, perhaps, why she wished to do so. Let him understand that there were far worse matters than a passing kindness to a friend! In a casual voice she said, "I see my aunt over there, Darry. Do you wish to meet her? I warn you she is not likely to fit with your notions of propriety."

His response was far beyond what she expected. Something that might have been contempt coloured his voice as he said, "Thank you, I have met her."

Puzzled but in too far to draw back now, Elisabeth said, "Well, I shall go over and say hello."

Before she could move, Darnell's hand shot out and gripped the reins of her horse in an iron hold. His voice scarcely above a whisper, he demanded, "Can you truly be so brazen? Care so little what might be said about you?"

This touched something within Elisabeth, and she said, "Letty is my aunt. However disreputable she may seem to you, she has always been a part of my life and I cannot just discard her as if she were of no importance."

"And yet you did not think your aunt of sufficient importance to speak of her to me before our wedding," he countered coldly.

"There ... there was not time," she stammered. "We married in such haste."

"And whose notion was that?" he demanded. She had no answer, and this time the contempt was open as he said, "So your father spoke the truth. And I was too trusting to believe him."

Elisabeth flinched as though she had been struck. "What did he tell you?" she asked in a whisper.

"Of your aunt and your closeness to her."

Darnell paused, then added, very deliberately,
"And of what occurred when you still lived at
home, with your father."

It scarcely seemed possible, but Elisabeth
turned paler than ever. She could not answer
and, without warning, turned her horse and
fled. Silently, stiffly, Darnell watched her go.
He was far too angry to follow or care what
attention she drew. All he could think of was
that what her father had said was the truth.

As for Elisabeth, she fled, scarcely able to
think, only knowing that she must get away.
The new house Darnell had hired for them
was deserted, save for the servants, and the
relative quiet seemed strange to her after the
activity of the viscount's townhouse. Today
she was more grateful than ever for the privacy,
for Elisabeth felt the need to think through
what had occurred. This was one time she
could not immediately go to Letty, and yet
there was no one else who could help her.
Around and around in her head went the knowledge that Darnell knew about her father and
what had passed between them and that he
hated her. Impossible to stay, and yet where
would she go? A sense of hysteria seemed to
overwhelm Elisabeth and she could only think
of escape. Finally, when she was calmer, she
was able to sit down and make plans. Hours
had passed, and still Darnell had not returned.
Good. That would give her the space to do
what she must.

With only the slightest regret, Elisabeth
looked at her closets and knew she could take
little from them on her flight. But then, she
had not married Darnell for clothes or trinkets
or the other luxuries he could give her. In that

moment Elisabeth knew that Mrs. Somerton must disappear and Harriet Tremaine once more appear. Well, she had lived that way once, and what difference did it make now? She could not marry anyone else, and if Darnell no longer loved her, it scarcely mattered what happened. Or so it seemed. Settled by having made her decision, Elisabeth rang for the maid and directed her to send up one of the servants Elisabeth had noticed was about her own size. That poor creature could only gape when asked if she had a plain cloak, dress, and bonnet she could give Elisabeth. The girl nodded, dumbfounded, and was too stunned to react further when her mistress went on to ask if she also had a small bag to carry belongings in. But she was also too well-trained to refuse, and soon Elisabeth had these things. The girl's greatest disappointment, no doubt, was that she was sworn to secrecy and, indeed, given the rest of the day off and directed to go out and "amuse herself." The girl would have been glad of the chance to gossip in the kitchen about the mistress's strange behaviour.

Soon enough, perhaps too soon, Elisabeth was ready. How grateful she was that there was no one to stop her and ask what she was about! For the servants were too new to take the liberty upon themselves to do such a thing, and there were no family members about to care. And so, as she had six years before, Harriet Tremaine set forth to find her place in the world. The greatest difference was that, this time, Miss Tremaine was not afraid of what she would find. She rather felt she would dislike it, but she was not afraid. And as she had years before, Elisabeth determined to make herself as difficult to find as possible. The answer to that, and to the need to set as much distance between herself and Darnell as she could, was to leave England. The continent was now quiet and she was certain that her Belgian employers would be pleased to help her find a new position. With a deep breath she set out for the inn where mail-coaches left for the coast. She would, she was determined, be out of London before nightfall. Fortunately, Darnell had replenished her purse just a few days before, and so she was beforehand with the world and need not panic if her plans went somewhat awry. What was, to Mrs. Somerton, mere pin money, was, to Miss Harriet Tremaine, a neat little nest egg that might take care of her needs for some time.

Behind her, Elisabeth left no note. Darnell might wonder where she had gone, but she could not believe he would greatly care. Not if her father had indeed told him tales. Better that Darnell forget her in bitterness than that she give him any clue which might help him to find her.

——17——

Darnell watched Elisabeth ride away and made no effort to stop her. Instead, he turned his horse toward the park entrance that would leave him nearest to his family's townhouse. He must, he felt, talk with someone who knew both him and Elisabeth, someone who valued her as much as he did. He could think of only one such person: his mother. She had taken a liking to Elisabeth and taken pains to draw her out over the past month or so, and Darnell knew she would listen and advise him. It was not a situation which pleased him, but he felt that if he could not speak with someone about what had occurred, he would go mad.

It was characteristic of Lady Langston that upon seeing Darnell, she at once directed the servants to tell any callers that she was not at home and that under no circumstances were they to be disturbed. Then she waited.

"Elisabeth and I have had a fight," he began directly.

"Of course." She nodded. He looked somewhat taken aback and she went on, "If you never had a quarrel, *that* would be cause for worry. Now tell me about the trouble."

Darnell did so, beginning with his encounter with Elisabeth on the *Golden Mermaid* and end-

ing with the fight he had had that day. When
he spoke of Elisabeth's father, he did not omit
his own impressions and dislike for the man.
Lady Langston was one of those expert listen-
ers who neither interrupted him nor allowed
her attention to wander.

When he had finished, Darnell said, "Well,
Mother? What shall I do? What do I believe?"

Lady Langston looked at her eldest son. With
care she chose her words. "I have always valued your judgement, Darry, and believe you
ought to, as well. If you wish more reassurance,
I remind you that your father and I have always considered Mr. Henrick something of a
bounder and I should not believe his word
above Elisabeth's."

"But she did not trouble to deny it," he
groaned.

"Did you tell her precisely what there was
to deny?" Lady Langston asked mildly.

"No," he said after a moment.

His mother looked at him calmly and said,
"If Elisabeth is indeed that poor girl you met
on the boat, then desperation must have driven
her to leave her home. Can you wonder she
does not like to speak of it? Or that she might
fear your reaction if she thought you knew of
her past? Go to her and talk of what has
occurred. Discover the truth. And only then
can you decide what to do."

"What . . . what if there is something in her
past I cannot forgive?" he asked, his voice
scarcely above a whisper.

"What if there is?" his mother repeated back
at him.

"I cannot give her up," he replied, white-faced.

Lady Langston's eyes twinkled at the despair in her son's voice. "If, in spite of all you find, you do not wish to give her up," she told him, "then trust yourself, for it means you ought not to. Forget what the *ton* might say. We Somertons are not sheep to follow tamely at all the rules society has made! We cannot afford to, unless we, too, wish to become sheep, and I, for one, do not."

Darnell laughed. "You are an original, Mother!"

"So I should hope," she agreed placidly. "And be frank with me. Was that not part of the reason you chose Elisabeth? Because she, too, does not fear to choose her own path?" She did not wait for his reply, only his smile. "Go on," she told him. "Go home and resolve this absurd contretemps."

Darnell smiled and rose. Then, as he turned to go, he stopped and said, "I am afraid to hurt her, Mother, by raising talk of things too painful for her."

Lady Langston gave her son a long clear look. "Elisabeth is not made of fragile porcelain," she said. "She will not shatter if you do."

Darnell did not go directly home. Indeed, it was very late when he returned to his own townhouse. Elisabeth, he thought, might be angry that his return had been so delayed that he was late for dinner. But surely that was better than if he had returned in time and they had once more fought. For time was what Darnell had needed to calm himself so that he could follow his mother's advice. Now he was prepared to face his wife again and tell her what he knew. Unfortunately, he did not get the chance.

The butler, who met Somerton at the door, held himself stiffly erect as Darnell said, "I presume my wife has already gone in to dinner?"

With only the slightest twitch of expression, the butler said gravely, "No, sir, Mrs. Somerton has not."

"Is she in her room?" Darnell asked, puzzled but not yet alarmed.

"I understand she is not."

"Did she go out?" Darnell persisted.

"As to that, sir, I cannot say for certain, but one must presume so, since she appears not to be in the house."

Stiffening, Darnell said, "Did she return, this morning?"

"Yes, sir."

"Did anyone speak with her, then?" Darnell asked, growing impatient with the obtuseness of the fellow before him.

"I believe an undermaid did, sir."

"Then let me speak with the girl, at once," Darnell demanded, abandoning all pretence of patience.

The butler bowed. "I regret, sir, that I cannot. It appears Mrs. Somerton gave the girl the rest of the day off and sent her out. We do not know where to find her," he concluded, anticipating Darnell's next question.

"I see." For a moment Somerton was quiet. Then he spoke curtly. "See that a small meal is prepared directly, one that can be packed and taken with me, if necessary. I may be going out."

"Very good, sir," the butler said, his voice as impassive as ever.

Darnell took the stairs two at a time until he reached the bedroom he shared with Elisabeth.

He looked about, seeing no greater disarray
than usual. Nor was there any note for him in
evidence. Calmer, now, he opened the doors of
her wardrobes, looking for signs that she had
taken any of her things, but he saw nothing
gone. So she had not, he concluded, run away.
That realisation gave him more relief than he
could express, and he sat in the nearest chair.
Where she had gone, he could not guess, but
the riding habit she had worn that morning lay
on the bed, so he knew she must have changed.
Perhaps she had told her maid where she was
going. Once more in command of his features,
Darnell rang for a servant and Elisabeth's maid
soon stood before him. She was a rather timid
woman, her timidity more pronounced than
ever on this occasion. Thinking to set her at
ease, Darnell said, "My wife has gone out and
I have stupidly forgotten what engagements
she had for this afternoon and evening. Did
she tell you where she was bound when you
helped her dress, earlier?"

"I did not help her dress," the woman sniffed.
"She chose to let an underservant do it. Or she
did it herself. I have not seen her since I dressed
her to go out riding, early this morning."

Thoughtfully Darnell stared at the woman.
Careful to keep his voice light, he said, "Do
you think that if you looked among her things
you could tell me which dress she wore? Then
I might recall where she was bound."

The woman nodded and began looking through
the crowded wardrobes. After several minutes
she turned back to Darnell and said, in a puzzled voice, "There doesn't seem to be a one of
her dresses missing, sir."

In that moment Darnell realised what must

have occurred. The matter was even more serious than he had first thought, if he was right.
With great difficulty he kept his voice steady
as he said, "Ah, I had forgotten! My wife had a
dress to be delivered, today. She must have
worn that. How stupid my memory can be, I
had altogether forgotten that. Well, I have my
own appointment for this evening. You may
go. Oh, and tell the kitchen I shall not want
that meal after all."

"Yes, sir," she said, sniffing with a patent
air of disbelief.

Darnell, however, was too preoccupied to
care. He was tired and hungry, but ignored
both. Instead, he hastily wrote a note for
Elisabeth. His guess might be wrong, or she
might return before he did. If so, he wanted
no further misunderstandings between them.

My dearest Elisabeth,
    I am more distressed than I can say by
what occurred between us this morning.
Please be assured that I love you and did
not mean much of what I said.
                                        Darnell

As soon as the note was sealed and laid upon
Elisabeth's pillow, Darnell was off, stopping
only long enough for a fresh horse to be brought.
He waited in the kitchen, astonishing and gratifying the cook by tasting one of her pastries
while he waited.

His clothes were not, he knew, precisely what
one was expected to wear when one calling
upon La Perdita, but Darnell did not care. If
he could not find Elisabeth there, he must be
prepared to ride after her. He hoped that La
Perdita could suggest where she might have

gone. Otherwise, he must trust to his own instincts.

La Perdita's major-domo was excessively well-trained. Very discreetly, but firmly, he informed the caller that Mrs. Roxbury was not receiving callers. His tone further implied that Mrs. Roxbury *never* received callers dressed as this one was. Unfortunately for the fellow, Darnell was in no mood to accept this very correct pronouncement. Curtly he thrust the man aside and told him, "Inform La Perdita—as discreetly as possible—that Mr. Somerton is here and wishes to speak with her at once." As the fellow bristled, Darnell went on, deliberately, "Further inform her that if she does not agree to see me, I shall visit her in her boudoir and I shall not be discreet about doing so."

The butler looked at Somerton, every inch the outraged servant. With disdain he turned and indicated that Darnell should wait in the book-room. "I shall see what I can do," he said coldly, then left the boorish visitor alone.

Although Somerton could not know it, this was a room Elisabeth had waited in, several times, dressed as the groom that so horrified Marietta. Instead, he silently pronounced it very comfortable and one he was surprised to find in the home of a woman such as La Perdita. Darnell had very little time with his thoughts, however, before an imperious Letitia Roxbury swept in on him. She wore the sheerest of robes and seemed not in the least distressed by the impropriety of receiving a gentleman in such attire. But then, Darnell reflected sardonically, La Perdita ought not to be.

"You wished to see me?" she demanded frostily.

"I do," he confirmed, a sardonic twist to his mouth. "Where is Elisabeth?"

La Perdita did not falter or stammer or evade, as Somerton half-expected her to do. Instead, she sat down in a chair directly facing him and said quietly, "She is not here, though it is evident you expected her to be. Why?"

"I am aware of her closeness to you," he replied bluntly, "and as I have reason to believe she has run away, I thought perhaps she had come to you. Has she?"

"Why did she run away?" Letitia asked, ignoring the question, her eyes hard and narrow.

"A curst fight," Darnell answered frankly.

"Over what?" Letitia persisted.

Somerton hesitated a moment, then said, "Over Elisabeth's past."

That brought a look of surprise to her face, and Letitia asked, in an altered voice, "What and how did you learn of her past?"

Evenly Darnell replied, "Her father came and spoke with me."

"And did you believe all that he told you?"

Letitia's eyes never left his face as he said, "I did not. And yet . . ."

"And yet you wondered," Letitia finished flatly for him. "Well, it was only to be expected." She paused and her eyes grew more piercing, though Somerton would scarcely have thought it possible. "What will you do if you find Elisabeth? Indeed, if you believe her father, why should you wish to do so?"

Darnell met her gaze squarely. "I love her. We must talk about the past, certainly, for I know about Harriet Tremaine. Indeed, I suspect that is how Elisabeth is now travelling, if she is not here. But I cannot believe that what-

ever the truth is, it will make me love her any
less. I cannot believe I have been so mistaken
in the honour and goodness I have felt in her."

For the first time, La Perdita smiled, and
the smile was a genuine one. "Well said, Mr.
Somerton. Very well, I shall help you. Elisabeth is not here, would that she were! But I,
too, must guess that she has dressed herself as
Harriet Tremaine and intends to once again be
a governess. Where she has gone I cannot be
sure. But she loves you and I cannot think she
will wish to be where she can see you, if she
truly intends to give you up. Nor where you
can easily find her. Did she leave no note?"

"None."

Letitia was silent for several moments. Finally she said, "I would wager she has gone for
the coast and means to sail for Belgium, where
she last held a post as governess."

Darnell rose. "Thank you," he said gravely.
"I must hope you are right. I shall go on the
coast road tonight and try to catch her before
she can sail. If I do not, I shall go on to the
continent. Can you give me the direction of
her last employers?"

Letitia immediately walked over to her desk
and wrote out the information for Darnell. As
she handed it to him, she said, "If we are
right, Elisabeth will most likely have taken the
mail coach and you should overtake it easily. If
you do, bring her to the estate I have given
directions to, below the address of the Belgian
family. I shall be there by midnight and perhaps,
together, we may sort things out."

For the first time Darnell smiled. He bowed
over Letitia's hand and kissed it. "Thank you,"
he said again. "I understand, now, why Elisa-

beth is attached to you." He paused. "I hope I have not caused you, er, trouble with your, er, guest?"

Letitia laughed and bit her lower lip. "You have," she answered frankly. "He will be cross as anything. But you needn't worry, I have had practice in soothing the foulest of tempers. And don't forget: I shall be at that retreat by midnight. Elisabeth is not likely to return with you unless she knows she will see me as well. Not if she chose to run away in the first place." La Perdita paused and added, "You *have* made a dreadful muddle of things, haven't you!"

Darnell smiled wryly. "I have," he agreed, "but I trust that between us we shall set it all right again."

"Don't doubt it," she retorted with mock sternness. "And now, be off with you!"

"I shall. Thank you and good-bye," he said.

"Good luck," was her reply.

—18—

Elisabeth found herself jolted and jostled about as the mail coach rattled its way to the coast. She had on one side of her a farmer's wife laden with a hefty basket of goods and on the other a thin, pale woman who tried in vain to hush her two crying children. Already one of the children had wandered away, at the last stop the mail coach had made, and now there was no chance that either would be permitted to descend from the coach for any reason until they reached their destination. This alone would have accounted for Elisabeth's headache, but it was spurred on by the presence of a corpulent cit, some minor merchant, no doubt, who seemed extraordinarily interested in the plain woman seated opposite him. He was not in the least deterred by the primness of her cloak or the ramrod straightness of her carriage. At the previous stop he had even offered to procure her a glass of wine if she wished it. Elisabeth barely suppressed a shudder. Two skinny clerks and an assortment of wild fellows on the roof completed the list of passengers travelling on the mail coach that night.

To be fair, the journey was no more unpleasant, the passengers no more distressing, than any she had known in the five years she had

travelled as Miss Harriet Tremaine previously.
It was amazing, Elisabeth could not help thinking, how quickly one becomes accustomed to
the luxury of a well-sprung carriage and the
courtesy of well-bred companions. Just a year
and a half ago Miss Harriet Tremaine would
have known how to depress, at a glance, the
pretensions of the cit. But Elisabeth was finding herself almost too tired to recall how it
was done. Nor did she seem to have the old air
of disdain that had come so naturally at such
times.

Moreover, then she had had no choice in her
journeys, and the decisions had always seemed
so clear-cut. But now, now she could not stop
her treacherous mind from remembering the
feel of Darnell's arms about her or the touch of
his lips upon hers. Even the thought of his
fingers gently stroking her neck was enough to
make Elisabeth shiver. Madness! she told herself with a determined shake of the head. Madness to even consider returning. You are Harriet
Tremaine! Harriet Tremaine. A governess. Plain
and meek and of no importance whatsoever!
Forget Darnell Somerton. Forget him and think
about what you shall say when you come face
to face with your old employers again. And
pray to God you are not yet breeding!

"Are yer bones aching, dearie?" the plump
woman beside Elisabeth asked her. "Mine always do. It's these confounded hard benches,
ye know. Have a cup o' tea at the next stop.
That'll fix ye up nicely. And if ye 'aven't the
change, I'll lend it to ye."

Elisabeth turned to look at the farmer's wife,
and for the first time since she had left Darnell
that morning, she smiled. "My purse is not yet

empty," she said quietly, "but you are very kind to offer. I shall have a cup of tea, I think, at our next stop. Do you know how soon that will be?"

"It's a bit of a while," the corpulent cit told her in a oily voice that made her very uncomfortable. "Don't worry, I shall tell you when we come upon it. And if you should wish a stronger restorative, I should be happy to procure it for you."

"What? A young woman like her trust herself to *yer* hands? Fie! She'll stay on her own and shame to ye for trying to seduce the poor thing," the farmer's wife told him bluntly.

The cit raised a hand in protest. "But I meant nothing by it," he swore. "Nothing but a wish to help."

"Help such as that she don't need," the woman told him with a snort.

At this point the cit lost his amiable expression. Looking directly at Elisabeth, he said, "The young woman will make her own choice and I'll thank *you* not to interfere."

"Interfere, is it?" the farmer's wife said with a strong sense of indignation. "A fine thing when a body can't look after a fellow body's needs!"

Somehow the cit managed to convey the suggestion of a bow. "Precisely," he said grimly.

To every passenger inside the coach it was evident that battle had been joined between the pair and the lines clearly drawn. Elisabeth, growing more and more distressed, now intervened. In a voice that was less forceful than she would have liked, she said, "I shall indeed make my own choices, sir. And they are to intrude my company on no member of this coach. I shall take tea and nothing stronger, and I shall take it alone."

Both the cit and the farmer's wife sniffed, but neither spoke, they simply glared at each other and at Elisabeth. Unable to cope any longer, she closed her eyes and prayed that they would soon reach the next stop and she might step out and breathe some air not filled with the smell of so many people crowded together.

And as the coach rattled along, Elisabeth slowly drifted into a restless sleep, one filled with angry dreams. All too soon, it seemed, someone was roughly shaking her awake. "No, Darry! Don't hurt me!" she cried out, still half-asleep.

"Aye, lovey, no one'll hurt ye now," a voice said comfortingly.

Slowly Elisabeth forced her eyes open, a hand against her throbbing forehead. "Where . . . where are we?" she asked, at last.

"The inn, dearie. The driver says we'll 'ave 'alf an 'our, at the least, and I thought ye could do wi' a cup o' tea."

Elisabeth looked around and discovered that everyone was looking at her expectantly. Her colour rising, Elisabeth said hastily, "Yes, of course. Thank you very much for waking me. Is it very late?"

One of the passengers looked out the now-open door of the mail coach. "Aye, the moon's been up an' all, though now it looks like it's coming on to rain. Best be hurrying, miss, if you want that tea. *If* they'll get it for you."

This last sounded ominous, but Elisabeth refused to be deterred. With dignity she allowed one of the clerks to help her down from the coach, and head held high, she entered the inn. There a kindly woman took one look at Elisabeth, listened to her request, and said, "Aye, we can do you a cup o' tea, but I'm thinking you'd like to freshen up a bit. 'Appens we've a room free you could use, aye, and take your tea there, as well. All that's open, down 'ere, be the bar, and I'm thinking that might seem a bit rough to you, ma'am."

Elisabeth felt far too ill to argue with such kindness, even if she had been inclined to. "Thank you," she said, for what seemed the hundredth time that evening.

Then, with what seemed the last of her strength, Elisabeth gathered her skirts and followed the woman up the narrow staircase. Ahead of her the candle the innkeeper's wife held flickered eerily, casting shadows upon the wall, and Elisabeth reflected that it was fortunate that she was not prone to imagining dangers where there were none. The room, when they reached it, proved to be small and, in the darkness, a trifle dingy. But Elisabeth was scarcely inclined to quibble when the woman had been so kind as to allow her to use it at all. Very soon she found herself alone there, with the few candles the woman had left lit for her. And finding herself alone for the first time in hours, Elisabeth gave way to her fears and exhaustion, making no effort to stem the flow of tears that overwhelmed her.

The innkeeper's wife, finding her in this state when she returned with the tea, said, "Ah, there now, you be tired, that I can see. Why not stay the night? There'll be another coach tomorrow and you can take it then. It be raining and I cannot think you'll like to travel in such a mess."

Elisabeth looked at her, hesitating. But after all, why not? She had the funds to do so and there was no need for such blind haste anyway. There was no way Darnell could ever guess where she had gone or find her. So, with what seemed akin to despair, Elisabeth said, "Yes. Yes, I should like to do that. Will you tell the coachman for me? And how much is the room?"

The woman told her and added, "I'll tell the coachman, though there's no true need. He'll simply go on about 'is way if you're not there when it's time to go."

Elisabeth watched the woman go, feeling altogether numb as she sank into a chair by the small table upon which the tea tray had been laid out. There were a few pastries and even a bit of cold ham to take away her hunger, a circumstance for which Elisabeth was grateful. Now that she had had a chance to rest a bit and cry, she found she needed nourishment and she fell to with a will. Perhaps it was this concentrated need that kept her from hearing the door of her room opening quietly. As her back was to the door, the first notice she had of the intruder was when an oily voice said, "Now that you've had a bite to eat, you'll be wanting company, I'll be bound!"

Elisabeth whirled to look at the man, the cit she had come to dread in the mail coach. "Get out of my room!" she cried, rising to her feet and backing away.

But the fellow only advanced towards her. "Now, now, lovey, is that a way to greet me? You're as lonely as I am, tonight, and why should we be alone? Come give us a kiss and you'll see how agreeable I can be."

Elisabeth backed farther away, feeling the old sense of dread sweep over her, paralysing her with fear. "Go away!" she whispered. "Just go away!"

But he would not. Just as her father had once done, he came closer, and Elisabeth could smell the whiskey on his breath. But this time there was no Letty to rescue her. Seizing the first object that came to hand, Elisabeth warned him, "I shall kill you if you so much as touch me."

The fellow laughed, not in the least deterred by the small vase Elisabeth had acquired. "Aye, I do like a bit of spirit in a girl," he told her with a low laugh. "A rare bit of fun we'll have, I tell you!"

Then, just as his hands reached for the bodice of her dress, Elisabeth saw the door of her room open and Darnell enter, his eyes large pools of angry colour and water dripping from his clothing. For the briefest moment he could only stare. Then, his voice rigid with anger he said, "Your amusements, madam, leave much to be desired!"

—19—

Darnell rode numbly, scarcely allowing himself to think, except at the inns where he stopped to ask after the mail coach. Then, having heard again that, aye, there was a drab mouse of a thing travelling that way, he would go on again. He did not waste time or effort in self-recrimination, time enough for that later, if need be. Now he needed his strength to find his wife. And when he did, he resolved that this time he would not make a muddle of matters.

And yet, Somerton was very tired when he finally did discover the inn Elisabeth had chosen to stay at. For the past several miles he had been riding a hired horse, and while it must be faster than a rattling mail coach, it was nevertheless not what he was accustomed to. When the rain began to fall, Darnell felt as if nothing more were wanting to set the seal of a disaster of a day. He would, he resolved, hire a post-chaise and four at the next halt, then press on overnight. In any event, if the disastrous weather held, Elisabeth would not be able to sail until the day after, at the earliest. So it was that Somerton reached the Horn and Hare Inn in the foulest of tempers. Curtly he asked for news of the mail coach and whether the inn could provide him with the post-chaise and four he needed.

"Aye, we've a carriage and four horses. Not the swiftest, mind, but dependable, and they'll carry a body safely on 'is way," the innkeeper answered slowly. "As for the coach, aye, it stopped 'ere. Been gone 'alf an 'our, I'd say. No space on it, anyway, sir. Full up, it was, tonight."

At that moment, the innkeeper's wife broke in to say, "No more it wasn't. Don't you mind you the girl that got off and is staying upstairs wi' us? Aye, and the gentleman from Lunnon that got off as well?"

"Oh, aye, now I do," he agreed slowly.

Impatiently Darnell broke in to ask, "What did she look like, this young woman? A brown mouse of a thing?"

The innkeeper's wife regarded him suspiciously. "Aye," she said grudgingly. "But wi' a way about 'er, almost like a lady, quiet and proper she seemed. What's your interest in 'er?"

Calmly Somerton lied, "She was a governess in my wife's employ and left without warning. We believe she took some of our silver with her and I mean to haul her back with me."

The innkeeper and his wife gasped. "Now fancy that!" she said, putting a hand to her breast. "And 'er such a sweet-seeming thing!"

"She is given to deceptions," Darnell replied grimly. "Will you show me where she is?"

"Oh, aye, sir. Shall we send for the constable? It be raining out and he'll not like to be called out on such a night, but when it's a matter of thieving . . ." the innkeeper said hesitantly.

Darnell bowed faintly and said in his haughtiest manner, "There is no need. I shall take the wench back to London and to justice there myself." He was, he realised, beginning to enjoy himself.

The pair seemed relieved and the innkeeper's wife promptly led the way upstairs. As he climbed, Darnell almost swayed with tiredness that came more from the strain of worry than physical fatigue. At the door of a room, the innkeeper's wife halted and said quietly, " 'Ere it is. Do you be wanting me to stay?"

Somerton looked at her and the nervousness in her face. "No," he said grimly. "I shan't need you."

Hastily she left him, going back down the stairs. Darnell waited until she was out of earshot and then opened the door before him. For a moment he could only stare, trying to grasp the sight that met his eyes. There, before him, Elisabeth was in the arms of a man! All his resolves melted before the sight and he could only close the door behind him and rap out, grimly, "Your amusements, madam, leave much to be desired!"

As he spoke, the fellow holding Elisabeth whirled to face him, and in the same moment she fainted. Stammering, he said, "I . . . I meant no offence, sir. Thought the lady might be lonely. I had no notion she was travelling with someone. I'll just be going along, now, and let you and the lady settle matters between you."

Contemptuously Darnell brushed past the fellow to where Elisabeth lay on the floor. Over his shoulder he said curtly, "Get out! And be grateful I shan't draw your cork for you!"

As fast as he could, the fellow did so. Darnell, kneeling on the floor over Elisabeth, gently lifted her head. As he did so, she began to come round. Somerton did not wait but lifted her to the nearby bed. Immediately she sat up in alarm. "Darry! What are you doing here? How did you find me?"

Darnell forced himself to step back and cross his arms against his chest, for otherwise they would treacherously have taken her in his arms. "I looked," he said steadily, "for a Miss Harriet Tremaine, *not* Mrs. Somerton."

Elisabeth flinched as though she had been struck. "Wh—who?" she whispered.

"Miss Harriet Tremaine," he repeated deliberately.

Her eyes fell. "So you know," she said. "Why, then, did you bother to come after me?"

"I know who you have been, but not why," he replied bluntly. "Will you tell me?"

Something stirred within Elisabeth and she looked up at her husband. "What need if you have already spoken with my father upon the matter?"

"I wish to hear from you what occurred." The voice and face were implacable. "And I shall not stir from here until you tell me."

"I see. I am to tell you everything?" she asked coolly.

He bowed. "You are."

With a bravado she did not feel, Elisabeth challenged, "And the man you saw here with me? You do not intend to ask about him?"

"In good time," was the uncompromising reply.

As Elisabeth stared at her hands, there

was a rap at the door. "Come in," Somerton called.

The door opened and the innkeeper's wife stood there. Disapprovingly she glared at Elisabeth, but her tone was respectful as she addressed Darnell. "Sir, my 'usband said to tell you the carriage is ready and waiting, though I must say it don't seem a kindly night to be travelling."

"C-carriage?" Elisabeth asked.

Silently Darnell cursed himself. To his wife he said, "I had forgotten I hired it when I first came in. Shall we stay the night, instead?"

"Stay the night?" the innkeeper's wife asked in outrage. "You're asking 'er?" She paused and her eyes narrowed, "You don't mean to share the same room, I trust, for I run a respectable inn 'ere and don't 'old wi' such goings-on! And what would your wife be saying, my fine gen'lemun, to learn you was sleeping wi' 'er governess?"

"Governess?" Elisabeth asked blankly.

The innkeeper's wife fixed her with a prim stare. "Well, what else do you claim to be? 'Is wife? He told us how you run away, taking with you what wasn't yours."

In spite of her weariness and dread, a flicker of laughter stirred in Elisabeth. In a voice that was not altogether steady she said to Darnell, reproachfully, "Was that needed, sir? To claim such a thing about me?"

"It was," he said curtly.

"Do you mean it isn't true?" the woman asked with rounded eyes.

Elisabeth looked at her hands and sighed mournfully. "Alas, it is true I was his governess, and that I ran away. But I stole nothing and left because he . . . he forced unwelcome attentions on me!"

The woman gasped. "Indeed! Fie on thee, sir!" To Elisabeth she added, "You needn't fear, dear, no harm shall come to you under *my* roof. In the morning the constable may sort the matter through."

Darnell stepped forward until he stood over his wife. With a grim smile he said, "I should prefer we left here tonight. *Letitia* is waiting for us." At the sound of her aunt's name, Elisabeth looked up at him in astonishment. With macabre satisfaction he went on, "Well? She is, I assure you, waiting for us."

"Where?" she managed at last.

He told her curtly, and with those words the resistance left Elisabeth. She knew very well the estate was one where Letty often went to rest and belonged to one of her oldest and most discreet admirers, Lord Croft. It was, in fact, the place where Letty had taken her when they first fled her father's house.

"I shall come," she said quietly. Then, with a grace and dignity the innkeeper's wife had not before seen her use, Elisabeth asked, "You need not fear, I shall be all right. How much do I owe you?"

A disapproving look on her face, the woman named an amount and waited as Elisabeth counted it out into her palm. Then, putting on her cloak and gathering up her reticule and small bag, Elisabeth turned to Darnell and said, "Shall we be going? I have no desire to cause Letty further concern."

Somerton nodded curtly and the innkeeper's

wife led the way. At the base of the stairs the innkeeper was waiting, no less pleased than his wife to be seeing the backs of the queer pair before him. And then they were out in the rain, Darnell helping Elisabeth into the carriage and directing the post-boy the way they must be going.

Only when they had set off, the sound of the horses hooves competing with the rain on the roof of their post-chaise, did Darnell give vent to some of his anger. "You have no desire to cause Letitia Roxbury further concern, but you seem to have no hesitation in doing so to me," he told her.

Elisabeth stared ahead in the darkness. "I had not thought you would follow me," she said quietly. "Or even that you would greatly wish to. I thought it better if you thought me gone and unfindable. Then you might go on with your own life without me to be a trouble to you."

"I see. And if you found you were breeding?"

She looked at him, her face in the shadows. "I should have returned then, if you wished it. For the child's sake I could have taken no other course."

"And by then you would have created quite a scandal," he observed tightly.

"I was angry and upset," she cried out, no longer able to stop herself. "What was I to do? Wait tamely at home for you to come and taunt me? What would that have resolved? Would it have been any less a scandal if I had run away later?"

There was no answer to that and Darnell did not try to give one. He was far too angry himself. Instead, he looked out the window at the darkness and the rain.

──20──

Letitia Roxbury stretched by the fire and watched as Lord Croft poured her a brandy. "I am delighted to see you, of course," he told her, handing her the glass, "but *why* are you here?"

Letty smiled at him, her eyes twinkling mischievously in a way that would have reminded Darnell strongly of Elisabeth. "I've come to impose dreadfully on you, Crofty. My niece, Lizzy, whom you know well enough, is coming here sometime tonight or in the next few days. At least I hope she is."

Lord Croft looked at her shrewdly. "A simple visit, eh? I don't believe it. And what of her husband? Didn't you tell me she had married that Somerton fellow?"

"So she did," Letty agreed complacently. "And Mr. Somerton will be coming with her."

"He is? Why?" Lord Croft demanded without rancour. "I understand him to have a very pleasant estate of his own, as well as the estates he will inherit when his father dies."

Letitia grinned at him. "Because I am an incurable meddler, my dear! Lizzy and her husband have had a dreadful spat and I intend to patch it up. But *not* on their ground, on mine. Or, rather, yours, Crofty. Do you mind?"

Lord Croft sat down opposite Letitia and for the first time it was possible to see that his eyes twinkled as merrily as hers. "Mind?" he demanded. "I should be disappointed if you had not thought of me. I confess I'm looking forward to seeing Elisabeth again. Lord, what a sight she was when you finally dressed her up and sent her off as an abigail, or whatever it was."

"Governess," Letty corrected him mildly. "Yes, she was. And much of that was Lizzy. I've always felt she had a certain flair and would have made a success of a career upon the stage." She paused and gave a mock sigh. "There are, you know, drawbacks to being respectable, Crofty, dear. Still, Lizzy has done well enough, particularly if we can patch up this silly quarrel!"

For several minutes Lord Croft was silent. Finally he said, "Look here, Letty, does Somerton *know* about Elisabeth's career as a governess?"

Letitia looked at him with eyes as shrewd as his own. "That, Crofty, is part of the quarrel. He's guessed, and my half-brother, John, has told him some tale as well."

Lord Croft shook his head. "A bad thing, all this, Letty. I didn't like it at the time and I don't like it any better now. Curst rum fellow, Henrick. Should have let me plant him a facer when I wanted to."

With affection, Letty regarded his Lordship. Croft fairly bristled with chivalry, made no less real by the fact that John Henrick outweighed him by several stone and always had. Indeed, it was unlikely Crofty could plant *anyone* a facer. But she only said, soothingly,

"Well, the past is over and done with. It is Lizzy's future we must look to, now."

Lord Croft nodded and replied, "Well, we shall see what we can do. My estate is yours for as long as you wish to stay here. In fact, if you would only agree, I should marry you and make it yours forever."

Letitia smiled but shook her head. "You know you would hate it, to be tied to me. Just as much as I should hate to be leg-shackled, even to someone as dear as you. We should be at each other's throats before a six-month was out!"

With a sad smile he said, "I doubt I should feel that way, but as you wish. You are far too beautiful and wild to ever be caged and I am content to have you when you will."

With the comfort of old friends they sat together, talking of past times, waiting for Elisabeth and Darnell to arrive. When the fire burned low in the grate, Lord Croft laid more logs on the hearth, not concerned that the servants were all asleep and he was required to do it himself. And when, at last, the clapper sounded at the front door, Letitia rose with him to go and answer it. There they found Darnell and Elisabeth standing in the rain, neither speaking to the other.

Suppressing a desire to smile, Lord Croft said with quiet courtesy, "Won't you please come in? My servants have all gone to bed, which is a beastly inconvenience, but I believe we can manage."

Elisabeth stood there silently, grateful that Crofty, as Aunt Letty always called him, had had the tact not to reveal to Darnell that he knew her. Darnell scarcely needed, she thought, any more surprises tonight.

With the same grave courtesy that Lord Croft had shown, Darnell responded first. "Thank you. Please go in, Elisabeth. I shall follow as soon as I have sent the post-boy to the nearest inn."

Lord Croft looked at Somerton in surprise. "Dismiss the fellow entirely," he said. "Tomorrow, or whenever you wish to leave, I'll warrant for it that we can find a carriage and horses for you. Certainly you may borrow mine or send for your own, as you choose."

Darnell smiled thinly. "Thank you. You are very kind."

As Somerton followed Lord Croft's advice, Letitia drew her niece inside. One glance had been sufficient to tell her that Darnell's guess had been correct and that Miss Harriet Tremaine had, indeed, been resurrected. "Well," Letitia said aloud, "you look as much the governess as ever! I only pray you shall not need to carry through this masquerade."

With feeling Elisabeth replied, "So do I, Aunt Letty! But at the moment I am afraid I may."

At this point Lord Croft interrupted to say, "No, dash it! I allowed it the first time, but I shan't again. If your husband is so much the fool he'll not keep you, I shall warrant for a place for you to stay."

From behind them came Darnell's voice, frigid with anger. "I am neither a fool nor a bounder. If Elisabeth and I are not able to patch up our quarrel, I shall still provide for her support."

For a long moment the two men stared at each other, neither giving way.

At last Letitia took matters into her own

hands. "It may be August," she said candidly, "but I shall *freeze* if we do not get back to that fire!"

Elisabeth laughed. "It is your own fault," she scolded. "Honestly, sheer muslin in the country?"

"Well, but Crofty has always liked me dressed this way," she protested. "Besides, it was the first thing that came to hand and I was in a hurry to be here."

Darnell did not look pleased by this interchange, but he said nothing, merely following the others into the elegant salon where La Perdita and Lord Croft had been waiting for them. Somehow nothing had gone the way he expected this whole mad day! Lord Croft, who was far shrewder than he looked, and indeed far shrewder than anyone gave him credit for, quietly poured a brandy for Darnell and a glass of ratafia for Elisabeth. Then he, too, waited.

Letitia watched as the players of the scene scattered themselves about the room. By necessity an excellent reader of faces, she soon had a tolerably good notion of what had transpired between Elisabeth and her husband. Therefore, it was not in blind faith that she said, her voice carrying easily throughout the room, "I should like to speak. You needn't regard Lord Croft save as a sort of member of the family. He wishes to help, as I do." Fixing her niece with a minatory eye, Letty said, "Since Elisabeth has never told you about her past, Mr. Somerton, it is time she did so."

It was difficult to say who was more startled, Elisabeth or Darnell. He, at any rate, recovered first. "I don't wish to hear any Banbury tales," he said darkly.

"Nor shall she tell you any," Letitia told him, meeting his eyes squarely. Then, deliberately, she looked at Elisabeth and said, "The time is past when silence will serve you, my dear. Your only recourse is the truth. All of it."

Slowly Elisabeth nodded, feeling as though she were in some sort of impossible dream, a dream that had become a nightmare and that one could not escape, one could only see it through.

An observer would have seen something very real. Four people in a comfortable room that was nevertheless far too large for them. Lord Croft was, perhaps, the one person most at ease, but he too felt a stake in what occurred. Over the years he had grown very fond of Letitia Roxbury, and that fondness had extended to Elisabeth the very first time he met her. For Lord Croft was not a man overly given to worrying about propriety. He simply knew when he liked someone. But he was well aware that his was a unique view among the *ton*. And for all his social activities, Somerton was a stranger to Lord Croft, and hence a man whose reaction to what Elisabeth must tell him could not be guessed. Whatever occurred, Lord Croft intended to see that no one was hurt, *if* that were possible.

Not unaware of the tension in the room, Letitia waited until it had reached an almost-unbearable pitch. Then she said quietly, "Lord Croft and I will leave so that the two of you may speak frankly with each other." She paused, then added, "You have no choice, Elisabeth. Your husband is, however, an honourable man and may even understand."

Then, as though to wait might change her resolve, Letitia nodded to Lord Croft and swept out of the room. He tamely followed, not in the least perturbed by Letty's high-handed disposition of his home.

After they were gone, there was a silence, broken at last by Elisabeth, who drew off her cloak and hat and set them aside. When that was done, she stood and faced Darnell, her back to the fire, unaware of the softness it gave to her face. "You have said, Darry, that you are somewhat acquainted with my father. And that you have heard of his reputation before he married?"

She clearly expected an answer and Darnell replied gravely, "I have. I have also heard that after his marriage there were no more scandals."

Elisabeth did not flinch from what he said, though her face had gone very pale. Instead, she continued to hold his eyes with hers and went on, "There were no more scandals because my father developed a taste for young girls. Girls without protectors to raise such scandals. My mother, moreover, aided him in suppressing any careless gossip that might otherwise have reached London." Elisabeth paused and drew a deep breath, her face pinched and drawn. "When I left school, my mother sent me on visits to family connections. But then she became ill and called me home. There—" Elisabeth broke off, unable to continue. She looked pleadingly at Darnell, but his face seemed to her harsh in its impassiveness. Finally, quietly, she went on. "My father was very certain that I would neither raise a scandal nor resist him. I mean to say that my father tried to . . . to ravish me. That he did not succeed was only because Aunt Letty was there, called in to settle some matter about my grandfather's estate. She was . . . she was in time to stop him from carrying out his intent. My . . . my father was not pleased. The things he said to us were intolerable and left no doubt that he meant to continue as he had begun: that he believed he was entitled to use me as he wished because I was his daughter. Nor would my mother protect me. There was no alternative save for me to leave my father's household. Unfortunately, there was nowhere else to go. My father made it very clear that if I ran away, he meant to pursue me, at whatever cost, and take me home again, to his grasp. Not one of my relatives could or would have protected me. Indeed most would have called me mad if I told them my story. My mother did.

"What was I to do? I could not go and stay with Letty! There seemed no choice but for me to yield up my name and take another. This I did. I became, as you seem to know, Miss Harriet Tremaine. With my hair done up plainly and dressed all in drab colours, I was altogether another person, the very humble, very timid governess in search of a new position. Aunt Letty was able to place me almost at once. And that was my life for five years. Until my mother died, leaving me a modest bequest. It was sufficient to allow Harriet Tremaine to disappear and Elisabeth Henrick once to more appear."

Elisabeth paused and her voice became harsh. "Not a pretty story, nor one that I could stand to have bruited about among the *ton*. As with my mother, there are too many who would hold me to blame."

Elisabeth watched Darnell's face, trying to read from it his thoughts. But Darnell changed nothing of his expression throughout the tale. The only clue for her was a certain grimness about his mouth and the shadows below his eyes.

At last he said, almost at random, "Your father told me there had been many men, that you threw your cap at them heedlessly. And that you were the same sort of woman as your aunt, La Perdita."

Elisabeth said, a wry, bitter smile upon her face, "As my Aunt Letty has often told me, I have neither the temperament nor a sufficient lack of scruples to follow in her footsteps! I find it far easier to imagine myself a nun." She paused and her tone became urgent as she said, "My father would tell any tale, any lie, to accomplish his ends. Indeed, he still thinks to have his way with me, for he could never bear to be thwarted."

His eyes dark pools of something Elisabeth could not read, Darnell asked her, curtly, "Why could you not tell me? If not before we were wed, then after?"

Elisabeth shook off the meekness and timidity that had seemed to grip her since their fight that morning. "How could I risk it?" she demanded quietly. "Is there one gentleman in a hundred, among the *ton*, who would have understood? One gentleman in a thousand who could have truly said it made no difference to him? I have heard all my life that what was said about me mattered more than the truth of who I am. And I have seen nothing to make me doubt that wisdom! What would *you* have done in my place? Would you have risked all

on the truth? I told you once that not everyone
could afford to play tamely at propriety all
their lives. Well, I tell you frankly, now, that I
have not. The lies my father has told you are
calumny, but even the truth would damn me
in the eyes of the *ton*. Can you tell me, now,
that it does not matter to you? That you are
prepared to forget what you have been told
and accept me as your wife? That what you
have heard has not given you a distaste of
me?"

Elisabeth paused and turned away. Her voice
was fierce as it came to him over her shoulder.
"You have no notion what it is to have lived
through what I have seen and had happen to
me! No notion of the terror of one's life when
one knows that such things have happened
once and could happen again. I cannot bear to
hear my father's voice again, inside my head,
telling me always that to speak of what he has
done is to damn myself as mad in the eyes of
the *ton*. What would you do, where would your
courage be, if you had found yourself threatened,
over and over again, with Bedlam? Would
you find it easy to speak of what occurred?
Easy to trust?"

Darnell could not help but flinch at the bitterness in Elisabeth's voice. Nor could he, in
honesty, deny the truth of what she said, nor
help but be shaken at the force of her fear,
which seemed almost to fill the room. And
because he could be honest, Darnell began to
understand what demon had pursued her and
kept her from trusting and confiding in him.
Nevertheless, he found that he, too, was shaking as he tried to speak. Elisabeth waited and,
when she realised that he could not yet reply,

spoke with a kind of proud bitterness. "I have done not one thing that I am ashamed of. But I am well aware you may not feel the same."

It was perhaps the quiet way in which she said these words that finally moved Darnell to his feet. "I do not blame you. Not for this, nor your father, nor the years as a governess. If I have trouble finding the words to answer you it is because I am appalled that anyone should have to bear such scars. If you still will have *me*, I still want you as my wife."

Elisabeth turned and found that Darnell stood directly behind her. Looking upward, her eyes met his steadily and she found that, after all this, still the matter was not decided. In a voice that held her determination Elisabeth said, "Do you? And what of the Duchess of Carston? Will you tell me the truth about her? For I tell you frankly that with that matter still between us, I cannot return to you. Whatever my past, I yet have the right to know about our future."

Darnell took Elisabeth's hands between his and led her to a nearby sofa, where he seated her beside himself. "I met Pamela years ago when she and I were much younger. She was in her first Season, in point of fact, and I almost as green. Pamela was all mad pranks and so unlike the other, insipid girls I had met. From the first time that I saw her I was in love with her, eager to offer her my hand in marriage. And I thought—" He broke off, his voice tinged with pain. With a breath, however, he recovered himself and went on, "I thought that she loved me. Indeed, she said so when I most improperly approached her before I spoke with her father." Now the bitterness crept in as Darnell explained, "Her father would not countenance the match. I was not wealthy enough or important enough to outweigh an earl. I tell you, Elisabeth, I was half-wild with anger and swore to Pamela that, if she wished it, I would carry her to the Scottish border and marry her over the anvil. Do you know, I thought she would come, but in the end, she did not. Instead, she married the earl, a fellow even older than her current duke. Can you imagine how I felt? I thought her father had forced her to the altar, and had my own father not stopped me, I think I should have called him out. And yet I stayed away from her, hoping if she wished it, Pamela would send for me. Perhaps I ought to have known better, but she was so bewitchingly beautiful and seemed so helpless. I know now, however, that she was not. Indeed, she managed me wonderfully well, never allowing me to cross the line and yet always making me feel that if she were not wed, she would be in *my* arms."

He broke off and stared at the fire for several long moments. Elisabeth did not dare break into his thoughts, and finally he went on. "Then the earl died and everything was wonderful. Or so I thought. She came with me to the continent, when Boney was still imprisoned on Elba. We were lovers and I pressed Pamela to marry me, again and again. She always refused, saying that she could not before her year of mourning was out. And then, suddenly, three months still shy of that date, she married the Duke of Carston. She was quite frank about it. More even than her father had, she wished to be allied to wealth and the highest title she could obtain, and so she married a duke rather than a mere future viscount. I was all cut up and swore I should never speak to her again. But she has not ceased to pursue me, determined to have her pleasure and her rank."

He stopped again and this time Elisabeth did not hesitate to ask, coolly, "And? Do you wait for her still?"

Darnell looked at his wife. In a voice that was as cool as her own he replied, "I have ceased, for some time now, to be the fool."

"Yet you kissed her."

"Yet I kissed her," Darnell confirmed. "She was gentle and sweet and said she wished me happiness upon my marriage and would I kiss her one last time? I did, and I will not pretend there was not an echo of sweeter times. But it was, I know, the echo of a young man's dreams, not an echo of the reality. I swear to you that Pamela is no threat to us."

Elisabeth digested this slowly. At last she said, "Why could you not tell me this when I asked?"

Darnell smiled wryly at her. "For the same reason you could not be honest with me. Fear and guilt. Fear that you would not understand. Guilt that anything had occurred at all."

She nodded. "How ironic that we should both so fear to speak!" There was a pause, and then she asked, "Why did you marry me, Darry? Was it because you recognised me as Harriet Tremaine or in spite of it?"

Darnell once more stared at the flames. "When I was younger, Elisabeth, I hated that my mother was so eccentric. And I swore to myself that I should marry a girl quite unlike her. As Pamela decidedly was. But as I grew older, and particularly after Belgium and the approach of Boney's armies, I found I understood why my mother was as she was and I found that I was tired of chits all froth and furbelows with no thoughts in their minds but of the next ball or what dresses they should wear. And when I met Harriet Tremaine on the boat, she was something I had not met before and I wished very much that she had been of the *ton* and not a governess. But she disappeared and I thought her lost forever. When I met you, the transformation was complete. I did not in the least suspect who you might have been; I only knew that in you, also, I had found a woman of character. And yet, you were also beautiful and gay and someone like myself. Soon I found I was in love with you and so I married you."

He paused. Elisabeth took a breath and asked in a rush, "When did you guess that I had been Harriet Tremaine?"

"When I kissed you, the first time, I knew. It was the day I asked you to marry me."

"Why didn't you speak?" she asked, determined to know the truth of the matter now.

He looked at her, troubled. "Because I did not wish to hurt you or scare you. And I hoped that you would come to me of your own accord and tell me what had occurred to make you take up such a mad masquerade."

"And yet you married me, anyway," Elisabeth said, a wondering tone to her voice. "And in such haste when I asked it of you."

Darnell nodded. It was his turn to ask the question. "Why did you want such haste?"

Elisabeth could not entirely suppress a shudder. "Because of my father. I had not seen him in six years and suddenly there he was, at Marietta's house in London, telling me that he meant to force me home with him. And that if any man asked his permission to wed me, he would refuse. He ... he threatened me with Bedlam if I should refuse to come home with him, giving me only a few days to consider his words. That was when I told you I would marry you. Only then, I thought, might I be safe. And later tell you everything, hoping you would understand." She looked down at her hands. "I loved you, you see. And before that, I felt I could not marry you without *first* telling you the truth, but at the same time could not bear to risk it. So I was caught, unable to do one or the other until my father's words overrode everything else." Earnestly she added, "I swear that even so I should not have wed you had I not been so in love with you."

Darnell looked down at her pleading eyes and in a moment his arms were around her and his lips closed over hers, the caress urgent and yet so completely reassuring.

A moment later, when he released her, Elisabeth asked, a mischievous glint in her eye, "Why, sir, don't you even wish to know about the fellow in my room at the inn?"

"Baggage!" he told her affectionately. "As though I had not guessed the fellow had thrust himself upon you and was unwelcome!"

Elisabeth looked at him uncertainly. "You did not seem to know it at the inn," she said, a hint of trouble in her voice.

Pulling her close again, Darnell said, "I was half-wild with worry by the time I found you, and past being able to know what I was seeing."

Once more the eyes twinkled. "Not, how-

ever," she told him severely, "too bewildered
to tell the innkeeper and his wife the most
outrageous Banbury tales! How could you?"

He grinned down at her. "Why I only followed *your* lead," he told her innocently.

Elisabeth made as though to hit him and
Darnell caught her hand in his and closed his
mouth again over hers. And it was as though
all the doubts and troubles between them had
never been.

—21—

Time seemed to stand still for Elisabeth and Darnell, caught up in a swirl of passion as fierce as any they had yet experienced. His breath coming hard and fast, Somerton let his hands explore the body that was so familiar and yet that still had the ability to surprise him. The clothing she wore frustrated him with its rows of buttons and high neck and many petticoats, but she was not the less attractive to him for it. With a reckless abandon that only made her seem more dear, Elisabeth reached up and loosed her hair from the pins that held it bound back so severely. Darnell buried his face in the chestnut cascade of sweetly smelling tresses. As he did, Elisabeth's hands reached for him, caressing his neck and back and even that most secret place in a way that promised so much pleasure. Only the dimmest perception that they were in a public room that might at any moment be entered kept them from completing their passion then and there. A fortunate precaution, for as they embraced, a voice coughed discreetly from the doorway.

Flushed and flustered, the pair sprang apart. At least Elisabeth attempted to do so. Darnell's arm held her too fast to entirely allow it. In

the doorway they saw Letitia Roxbury and Lord
Croft grinning at them rather happily. Coming
forward, Letty said, in a dry voice, "I gather
you have patched up your quarrel. Splendid. I
trust nothing has been held back?" she asked,
fixing her niece with a piercing stare.

"Nothing," Elisabeth confirmed, still blushing fiercely.

"Good!" Letitia said briskly. "I still cannot
believe the pair of you made such a desperate
muddle of it in the first place!"

Lord Croft nodded his head. "A dasht good
thing you've patched it up, too! The question,
now, is, what to do with you? The servants
have all gone to bed and none of the rooms
were prepared in advance."

Darnell coloured. "Perhaps I ought not to
have sent off the post-boy."

Lord Croft waved a hand carelessly. "Nonsense! We shall contrive. We always have.
Nevertheless, it is a bit of a puzzle. Letty and I
have often sat up the night, but that won't do
for the pair of you. Even if you weren't smelling of April and May, you both look as though
you could use a rest. What shall we do, Letitia?"

Affectionately she took his arm. "Don't fret,
Crofty. They shall, of course, use, er, my room.
And we shall, as we often have, sit up and talk
of old times past and exchange, between us,
the most shocking gossip! Will that do?" she
asked her niece.

Darnell and Elisabeth exchanged the briefest of glances and a smile lurked in their eyes.
"It will do," she confirmed.

"Good!" Letty said, again briskly. "You'll
find that mine is the fourth room on the right
as you come off the second-floor stairs. Take

this candle and you shall have no trouble finding the way. The room is done all in red."

"Thank you," Elisabeth said shyly, and took the proffered candle.

Somerton was more at his ease. One possessive arm still firmly fixed about his wife's waist, he nevertheless bowed over Letty's hand and said, "I am very grateful to you, ma'am, and am forever your servant."

Letitia Roxbury smiled with satisfaction but made no effort to detain the pair further. Indeed, they had reached the doorway of the salon before she said, in a voice that was a trifle hesitant, "You might wish to know, my dears, that the room is, er, entirely soundproofed. That is, you need not feel any concern as to what the servants might hear."

In a rather haughty tone Darnell replied, "Indeed? The matter is, I assure you, one of indifference to me."

Helpless to stop herself, Elisabeth said mischievously, in a disappointed voice, "Really, Darry? I had no notion you meant only to go to sleep. I have been thoroughly deceived in you!"

At that, Darnell coloured. "Baggage!" he retorted hastily. "Upstairs with you, now."

With an effort, Letty restrained her laughter and turned toward Lord Croft, not wishing to embarrass Darnell and her niece further. When they were gone, however, she and Crofty smiled knowingly at each other. "I do think they shall enjoy themselves, up there," she told him, with a satisfied sigh. "Shall *we* go and use the swing in *your* room, my dearest Crofty? I should so like to show my appreciation."

Lord Croft looked at the bewitching woman beside him and smiled. "Why not?" he replied, his smile as delighted as her own. "Why else do you think I keep it there? Let us only hope we don't scandalise your niece's husband, in the morning."

"Morning!" Letitia laughed. "My dear Crofty, I shall be amazed if we see them before supper!"

JOIN THE REGENCY READERS' PANEL

Help us bring you more of the books you like by filling out this survey and mailing it in today.

1. Book title:_____

   Book #:_____

2. Using the scale below how would you rate this book on the following features.

Poor		Not so Good			O.K.			Good		Excel- lent
0	1	2	3	4	5	6	7	8	9	10

Rating

Overall opinion of book . . . . _____
Plot/Story . . . . _____
Setting/Location . . . . _____
Writing Style . . . . _____
Character Development . . . . _____
Conclusion/Ending . . . . _____
Scene on Front Cover . . . . _____

3. On average about how many romance books do you buy for

   yourself each month?_____

4. How would you classify yourself as a reader of Regency romances?
   I am a ( ) light ( ) medium ( ) heavy reader.

5. What is your education?
   ( ) High School (or less) ·   ( ) 4 yrs. college
   ( ) 2 yrs. college   ( ) Post Graduate

6. Age_____   7. Sex: ( ) Male ( ) Female

Please Print Name_____

Address_____

City_____State_____Zip_____

Phone # (   )_____

Thank you. Please send to New American Library, Research Dept, 1633 Broadway, New York, NY 10019.

SIGNET Regency Romances You'll Enjoy